THE MURDERED MAN'S WIDOW
WAS AN ALLURING WOMAN

Adele Fortescue's appeal was obvious, not subtle. It simply said to every man, "Here I am. I'm a woman." She spoke and moved and breathed sex. . . .

"I've been trying to get in touch with you since this morning," Inspector Neele said. "Your husband was taken to St. Jude's Hospital."

"You don't mean—he isn't—dead?" She fumbled with her bag, pulled out a handkerchief and sobbed in a manner that was almost convincing.

"I'll send someone to you," said Inspector Neele, watching her closely as he went to the door. She likes men, he thought, but she'll always like money better. The handkerchief did not quite obscure her mouth. On her lips, he noted, there was a very faint smile.

Agatha Christie

A Pocket Full of Rye

PUBLISHED BY POCKET BOOKS NEW YORK

The characters and situations in this book are wholly
fictional and imaginative: they do not portray and are
not intended to portray any actual persons or parties.

**POCKET BOOKS, a Simon & Schuster division of
GULF & WESTERN CORPORATION
1230 Avenue of the Americas, New York, N.Y. 10020**

Copyright 1953 by The Copyright Trading Company, Ltd.

Published by arrangement with Dodd, Mead & Company

ISBN: 0-671-43462-4

First Pocket Books printing January, 1955

20   19   18   17   16

POCKET and colophon are trademarks of Simon & Schuster.

Printed in the U.S.A.

Cast of Characters

REX FORTESCUE—who drinks his last cup of tea and is found with a pocket full of rye.

INSPECTOR NEELE—a man whose appearance belies his shrewdness.

CRUMP—butler at Fortescue's Yewtree Lodge who tipples a bit.

MARY DOVE—efficient, self-possessed housekeeper, who seems amused by the tragic drama at Yewtree.

SERGEANT HAY—Inspector Neele's leg man.

GLADYS MARTIN—the Lodge's not-too-bright parlormaid.

MRS. CRUMP—cook at Yewtree who takes pride in her work.

LANCELOT FORTESCUE—Rex's prodigal son, brilliant black sheep of the family.

PAT FORTESCUE—his wife, who is more at home with horses than with the Fortescues.

ADELE FORTESCUE—Rex's attractive second wife, who, gossips say, married for money.

VIVIAN DUBOIS—Adele's cautious "golf partner."

JENNIFER FORTESCUE—Percival's wife, a plump and pasty perennial London shopper.

ELLEN—housemaid, whose mother told her never to touch yew berries.

MISS RAMSBOTTOM—Rex's sister-in-law, who wants no truck with sin and wickedness.

ELAINE FORTESCUE—Rex's daughter, the only one of the clan who shows genuine grief.

PERCIVAL FORTESCUE—Rex's son and business partner, prim and fastidious but by no means stupid.

MISS MARPLE—elderly but sharp-witted lady with a notion about blackbirds.

GERALD WRIGHT—schoolmaster, unofficially engaged to Elaine.

A Pocket
Full of Rye

Chapter One

It was Miss Somers' turn to make the tea. Miss Somers was the newest and the most inefficient of the typists. She was no longer young and had a mild worried face like a sheep. The kettle was not quite boiling when Miss Somers poured the water onto the tea, but poor Miss Somers was never quite sure when a kettle was boiling. It was one of the many worries that afflicted her in life.

She poured out the tea and took the cups round with a couple of limp sweet biscuits in each saucer.

Miss Griffith, the efficient head typist, a gray-haired martinet who had been with Consolidated Investments Trust for sixteen years, said sharply: "Water not boiling again, Miss Somers!" and Miss Somers' worried meek face went pink and she said, "Oh dear, I did think it was boiling this time."

Miss Griffith thought to herself: "She'll last for another month, perhaps, just while we're so busy. . . . But really! The mess the silly idiot made of that letter to Eastern Developments—a perfectly straightforward job, and always so stupid over the tea. If it weren't so difficult to get hold of any intelligent typists—and the biscuit tin lid wasn't shut tightly last time, either. Really—"

Like so many of Miss Griffith's indignant inner communings, the sentence went unfinished.

At that moment Miss Grosvenor sailed in to make Mr. Fortescue's sacred tea. Mr. Fortescue had different tea, and different china and special biscuits. Only the kettle and the water from the cloakroom tap were the same. But on this occasion, being Mr. Fortescue's tea, the water boiled. Miss Grosvenor saw to that.

Miss Grosvenor was an incredibly glamorous blonde. She wore an expensively cut little black suit and her shapely legs were encased in the very best and most expensive black-market nylons.

She sailed back through the typists' room without deigning to give anyone a word or a glance. The typists might have been so many black beetles. Miss Grosvenor was Mr. Fortescue's own special personal secretary; unkind rumor always hinted that she was something more, but actually this was not true. Mr. Fortescue had recently married a second wife, both glamorous and expensive, and fully capable of absorbing all his attention. Miss Grosvenor was to Mr. Fortescue just a necessary part of the office décor, which was all very luxurious and very expensive.

Miss Grosvenor sailed back with the tray held out in front of her like a ritual offering. Through the inner office and through the waiting room, where the more important clients were allowed to sit, and through her own anteroom and finally with a light tap on the door she entered that holy of holies, Mr. Fortescue's office.

It was a large room with a gleaming expanse of parquet floor on which were dotted expensive oriental rugs.

It was delicately paneled in pale wood and there were some enormous stuffed chairs upholstered in pale buff leather. Behind a colossal sycamore desk, the center and focus of the room, sat Mr. Fortescue himself.

Mr. Fortescue was less impressive than he should have been to match the room, but he did his best. He was a large flabby man with a gleaming bald head. It was his affectation to wear loosely-cut country tweed in his city office. He was frowning down at some papers on his desk when Miss Grosvenor glided up to him in her swan-like manner. Placing the tray on the desk at his elbow, she murmured in a low impersonal voice, "Your tea, Mr. Fortescue," and withdrew.

Mr. Fortescue's contribution to the ritual was a grunt.

Seated at her own desk again, Miss Grosvenor proceeded with the business in hand. She made two telephone calls, corrected some letters that were lying there typed ready for Mr. Fortescue to sign, and took one incoming call.

"Ay'm afraid it's impossible just now," she said in haughty accents. "Mr. Fortescue is in conference."

As she laid down the receiver she glanced at the clock. It was ten minutes past eleven.

It was just then that an unusual sound penetrated through the almost soundproof door of Mr. Fortescue's office. Muffled, it was yet fully recognizable, a strangled, agonized cry. At the same moment the buzzer on Miss Grosvenor's desk sounded in a long-drawn, frenzied summons. Miss Grosvenor, startled for a moment into complete immobility, rose uncertainly to her feet. Confronted by the unexpected, her poise was shaken. However, she moved towards Mr. Fortescue's door in her usual statuesque fashion, tapped and entered.

What she saw upset her poise still further. Her employer behind his desk seemed contorted with agony. His convulsive movements were alarming to watch.

Mss Grosvenor said, "Oh dear, Mr. Fortescue, are you ill?" and was immediately conscious of the idiocy of the question. There was no doubt that Mr. Fortescue was very seriously ill. Even as she came up to him, his body was convulsed in a painful, spasmodic movement.

Words came out in jerky gasps.

"Tea—what the hell—you put in the tea—get help—quick, get a doctor—"

Miss Grosvenor fled from the room. She was no longer the supercilious blonde secretary. She was a thoroughly frightened woman who had lost her head.

She came running into the typists' office crying out, "Mr. Fortescue's having a fit—he's dying—we must get a doctor—he looks awful—I'm sure he's dying."

Reactions were immediate, and varied a good deal.

Miss Bell, the youngest typist, said, "If it's epilepsy we ought to put a cork in his mouth. Who's got a cork?"

Nobody had a cork.

Miss Somers said, "At his age it's probably apoplexy."

Miss Griffith said, "We must get a doctor—at once."

But she was hampered in her usual efficiency because in all her sixteen years of service it had never been necessary to call a doctor to the city office. There was her own doctor but that was at Streatham Hill. Where was there a doctor near here?

Nobody knew. Miss Bell seized a telephone directory and began looking up Doctors under D. But it was not a classified directory, and doctors were not automatically listed like taxis. Someone suggested a hospital, but which hospital? "It has to be the right hospital," Miss Somers insisted, "or else they won't come. Because of the National Health, I mean. It's got to be in the area."

Someone suggested that she dial Emergency at 999 but Miss Griffith was shocked at that and said it would mean the police and that would never do. For citizens of a country which enjoyed the benefits of Medical Service for all, a group of quite reasonably intelligent women showed incredible ignorance of correct procedure. Miss Bell started looking up Ambulances under A. Miss Griffith said, "There's his own doctor—he must have a doctor." Someone rushed for the private address book. Miss Griffith instructed the office boy to go out and find a doctor—somehow, anywhere. In the private address book, Miss Griffith found Sir Edwin Sandeman with an address in Harley Street. Miss Grosvenor, collapsed in a chair, wailed in a voice whose accent was noticeably less Mayfair than usual, "I made the tea just as usual—reely I did—there couldn't have been anything wrong in it. . . ."

"Wrong in it?" Miss Griffith paused, her hand on the dial of the telephone. "Why do you say that?"

"He said it—Mr. Fortescue—he said it was the tea—"

Miss Griffith's hand hovered irresolutely between Welbeck and 999. Miss Bell, young and hopeful, said: "We ought to give him some mustard and water—now. Isn't there any mustard in the office?"

There was no mustard in the office.

Some short while later Dr. Isaacs of Bethnal Green and Sir Edwin Sandeman met in the elevator just as two different ambulances drew up in front of the building. The telephone and the office boy had done their work.

Chapter Two

Inspector Neele sat in Mr. Fortescue's sanctum behind Mr. Fortescue's vast sycamore desk. One of his underlings with a notebook sat unobtrusively against the wall near the door.

Inspector Neele had a smart, soldierly appearance with crisp brown hair growing back from a rather low forehead. When he uttered the phrase "just a matter of routine" those addressed were wont to think spitefully: "And routine is about all you're capable of!" They would have been quite wrong. Behind his unimaginative appearance, Inspector Neele was a highly imaginative thinker, and one of his methods of investigation was to propound to himself fantastic theories of guilt which he applied to such persons as he was interrogating at the time.

Miss Griffith, whom he had at once picked out with an unerring eye as being the most suitable person to give him a succinct account of the events which had led to his being seated where he was, had just left the room, having given him an admirable résumé of the morning's happenings. Inspector Neele propounded to himself three separate, highly colored reasons why the faithful *doyenne* of the typists' room should have poisoned her employer's mid-morning cup of tea, and rejected them as unlikely.

He classified Miss Griffith as (*a*) not the type of a poisoner; (*b*) not in love with her employer; (*c*) no pronounced mental instability; (*d*) not a woman who cherished grudges. That really seemed to dispose of Miss Griffith except as a source of accurate information.

Inspector Neele glanced at the telephone. He was expecting a call from St. Jude's Hospital at any moment now.

It was possible, of course, that Mr. Fortescue's sudden illness was due to natural causes, but Dr. Isaacs of Bethnal Green had not thought so and Sir Edwin Sandeman of Harley Street had not thought so.

Inspector Neele pressed a buzzer conveniently situated at his left hand and demanded that Mr. Fortescue's personal secretary should be sent in to him.

Miss Grosvenor had recovered a little of her poise, but not much. She came in apprehensively, with nothing of the swanlike glide about her motions, and said at once defensively:

"I didn't do it!"

Inspector Neele murmured conversationally: "No?"

He indicated the chair where Miss Grosvenor was wont to place herself, pad in hand, when summoned to take down Mr. Fortescue's letters. She sat down now with reluctance and eyed Inspector Neele in alarm. Inspector Neele, his mind playing imaginatively on the themes—Seduction? Blackmail? Platinum Blonde in Court?, etc.—looked reassuring and just a little stupid.

"There wasn't anything wrong with the tea," said Miss Grosvenor. "There couldn't have been."

"*I* see," said Inspector Neele. "Your name and address, please?"

"Grosvenor. Irene Grosvenor."

"How do you spell it?"

"Oh. Like the Square."

"And your address?"

"14 Rushmoor Road, Muswell Hill."

Inspector Neele nodded in satisfied fashion.

"No seduction," he said to himself "No Love Nest. Respectable home with parents. No blackmail."

Another good set of speculative theories washed out.

"And so it was you who made the tea?" he said pleasantly.

"Well, I had to. I always do, I mean."

Unhurried, Inspector Neele took her closely through the morning ritual of Mr. Fortescue's Tea. The cup and saucer and teapot had already been packed up and dispatched to the appropriate quarter for analysis. Now Inspector Neele learned that Irene Grosvenor and only Irene Grosvenor had handled that cup and saucer and teapot. The kettle had been used for making the office tea and had been refilled from the cloakroom tap by Miss Grosvenor.

"And the tea itself?"

"It was Mr. Fortescue's own tea, special China tea. It's kept on the shelf in my room next door."

Inspector Neele nodded. He inquired about sugar and heard that Mr. Fortescue didn't take sugar.

The telephone rang. Inspector Neele picked up the receiver. His face changed a little.

"St. Jude's?"

He nodded to Miss Grosvenor in dismissal.

"That's all for now, thank you, Miss Grosvenor."

Miss Grosvenor sped out of the room hurriedly.

Inspector Neele listened carefully to the thin, unemotional tones speaking from St. Jude's Hospital. As the voice spoke he made a few cryptic signs with a pencil on the corner of the blotter in front of him.

"Died five minutes ago, you say?" he asked. His eye went to the watch on his wrist. Twelve forty-three, he wrote on the blotter.

The unemotional voice said that Doctor Bernsdorff himself would like to speak to Inspector Neele.

Inspector Neele said, "Right. Put him through," which rather scandalized the owner of the voice who had allowed a certain amount of reverence to seep into the official accents.

There were then various clicks, buzzes, and far-off ghostly murmurs. Inspector Neele sat patiently waiting.

Then without warning a deep bass roar caused him to shift the receiver an inch or two away from his ear.

"Hullo, Neele, you old vulture. At it again with your corpses?"

Inspector Neele and Professor Bernsdorff of St. Jude's had been brought together over a case of poisoning just over a year ago and had remained on friendly terms.

"Our man's dead, I hear, Doc."

"Yes. We couldn't do anything by the time he got here."

"And the cause of death?"

"There will have to be an autopsy, naturally. Very interesting case. Very interesting indeed. Glad I was able to be in on it."

The professional gusto in Bernsdorff's rich tones told Inspector Neele one thing, at least.

"I gather you don't think it was natural death," he said dryly.

"Not a dog's chance of it," said Dr. Bernsdorff robustly. "I'm speaking unofficially, of course," he added with belated caution.

"Of course. Of course. That's understood. He was poisoned?"

"Definitely. And what's more—this is quite unofficial, you understand—just between you and me—I'd be prepared to make a bet on what the poison was."

"In-deed?"

"Taxine, my boy. Taxine."

"Taxine? Never heard of it."

"I know. Most unusual. Really delightfully unusual! I don't say I'd have spotted it myself if I hadn't had a case only three or four weeks ago. Couple of kids playing dolls' tea-parties—pulled berries off a yew tree and used them for tea."

"Is that what it is? Yew berries?"

"Berries or leaves. Highly poisonous. Taxine, of course, is the alkaloid. Don't think I've heard of a case where it was used deliberately. Really most interesting and unusual. . . . You've no idea, Neele, how tired one gets of the inevitable weedkiller. Taxine is a real treat. Of course, I may be wrong—don't quote me, for Heaven's sake—but I don't think so. Interesting for you, too, I should think. Varies the routine!"

"A good time is to be had by all, is that the idea? With the exception of the victim."

"Yes, yes, poor fellow." Dr. Bernsdorff's tone was perfunctory. "Very bad luck on him."

"Did he say anything before he died?"

"Well, one of your fellows was sitting by him with a notebook. He'll have the exact details. He muttered something once about tea—that he'd been given something in his tea at the office—but that's nonsense, of course."

"Why is it nonsense?" Inspector Neele, who had been reviewing speculatively the picture of the glamorous

Miss Grosvenor adding yew berries to a brew of tea, and finding it incongruous, spoke sharply.

"Because the stuff couldn't possibly have worked so soon. I understand the symptoms came on immediately after he had drunk the tea?"

"That's what they say."

"Well, there are very few poisons that act as quickly as that, apart from the cyanides, of course—and possibly pure nicotine—"

"And it definitely wasn't cyanide or nicotine?"

"My dear fellow. He'd have been dead before the ambulance arrived. Oh no, there's no question of anything of that kind. I did suspect strychnine, but the convulsions were not at all typical. Still unofficial, of course, but I'll stake my reputation it's taxine."

"How long would that take to work?"

"Depends. An hour. Two hours, three hours. Deceased looked like a hearty eater. If he had a big breakfast, that would slow things up."

"Breakfast," said Inspector Neele thoughtfully. "Yes, it looks like breakfast."

"Breakfast with the Borgias." Dr. Bernsdorff laughed cheerfully. "Well, good hunting, my lad."

"Thanks, doctor. I'd like to speak to my sergeant before you ring off."

Again there were clicks and buzzes and far-off ghostly voices. And then the sound of heavy breathing came through, an inevitable prelude to Sergeant Hay's conversation.

"Sir," he said urgently. "Sir."

"Neele here. Did the deceased say anything I ought to know?"

"Said it was the tea. The tea he had at the office. But the Medical Officer says not . . ."

"Yes, I know about that. Nothing else?"

"No, sir. But there's one thing that's odd. The suit

he was wearing—I checked the contents of the pockets. The usual stuff—handkerchief, keys, change, wallet—but there was one thing that's downright peculiar. The right-hand pocket of his jacket. It had cereal in it."

"Cereal?"

"Yes, sir."

"What do you mean by cereal? Do you mean a breakfast food? Farmer's Glory or Wheatifax? Or do you mean corn or barley—"

"That's right, sir. Grain it was. Looked like rye to me. Quite a lot of it."

"I see. . . . Odd. . . . But it might have been a sample—something to do with a business deal."

"Quite so, sir—but I thought I'd better mention it."

"Quite right, Hay."

Inspector Neele sat staring ahead of him for a few moments after he had replaced the telephone receiver. His orderly mind was moving from Phase I to Phase II of the inquiry—from suspicion of poisoning to certainty of poisoning. Professor Bernsdorff's words may have been unofficial, but Professor Bernsdorff was not a man to be mistaken in his beliefs. Rex Fortescue had been poisoned and the poison had probably been administered one to three hours before the onset of the first symptoms. It seemed probable, therefore, that the office staff could be given a clean bill of health.

Neele got up and went into the outer office. A little desultory work was being done but the typewriters were not going at full speed.

"Miss Griffith? Can I have another word with you?"

"Certainly, Mr. Neele. Could some of the girls go out to lunch? It's long past their regular time. Or would you prefer that we get something sent in?"

"No. They can go to lunch. But they must return afterwards."

"Of course."

Miss Griffith followed Neele back into the private office. She sat down in her composed efficient way.

Without preamble, Inspector Neele said, "I have heard from St. Jude's Hospital. Mr. Fortescue died at 12:43."

Miss Griffith received the news without surprise, merely shook her head.

"I was afraid he was very ill," she said.

She was not, Neele noted, at all distressed.

"Will you please give me particulars of his home and family?"

"Certainly. I have already tried to get into communication with Mrs. Fortescue, but it seems she is out playing golf. She was not expected home to lunch. There is some uncertainty as to which course she is playing on." She added in an explanatory manner, "They live at Baydon Heath, you know, which is a center for three well-known golf courses."

Inspector Neele nodded. Baydon Heath was almost entirely inhabited by rich city men. It had an excellent train service, was only twenty miles from London and was comparatively easy to reach by car even in the rush of morning and evening traffic.

"The exact address, please, and the telephone number?"

"Baydon Heath 3400. The name of the house is Yewtree Lodge."

"*What?*" The sharp query slipped out before Inspector Neele could control it. "Did you say Yewtree Lodge?"

"Yes."

Miss Griffith looked faintly curious, but Inspector Neele had himself in hand again.

"Can you give me particulars of his family?"

"Mrs. Fortescue is his second wife. She is much younger than he is. They were married about two years ago. The first Mrs. Fortescue has been dead a long time. There are two sons and a daughter of the first marriage. The daughter lives at home and so does the elder son who is a partner in the firm. Unfortunately he is away in the North of England today on business. He is expected to return tomorrow."

"When did he go away?"

"The day before yesterday."

"Have you tried to get in touch with him?"

"Yes. After Mr. Fortescue was removed to the hospital I rang up the Midland Hotel in Manchester where I thought he might be staying, but he had left early this morning. I believe he was also going to Sheffield and Leicester, but I am not sure about that. I can give you the names of certain firms in those cities which he might be visiting."

Certainly an efficient woman, thought the Inspector, and if she murdered a man she would probably murder him very efficiently, too. But he forced himself to abandon these speculations and concentrate once more on Mr. Fortescue's home front.

"There is a second son, you said?"

"Yes. But owing to a disagreement with his father he lives abroad."

"Are both sons married?"

"Yes. Mr. Percival has been married for three years. He and his wife occupy a self-contained flat in Yewtree Lodge, though they are moving into their own house at Baydon Heath very shortly."

"You were not able to get in touch with Mrs. Percival Fortescue when you rang up this morning?"

"She had gone to London for the day." Miss Griffith went on, "Mr. Lancelot got married less than a year ago. To the widow of Lord Frederick Anstice. I expect you've seen pictures of her. In the *Tatler*—with horses, you know. And at point to points."

Miss Griffith sounded a little breathless and her cheeks were faintly flushed. Neele, who was quick to catch the moods of human beings, realized that this marriage had thrilled the snob and the romantic in Miss Griffith. The aristocracy was the aristocracy to Miss Griffith, and the fact that the late Lord Frederick Anstice had had a somewhat unsavory reputation in sporting circles was almost certainly not known to her. Freddie Anstice had blown his brains out just before an inquiry by the Stewards into the running of one of his horses. Neele remembered something vaguely about his wife. She had been the daughter of an Irish peer and had been married before to an airman who had been killed in the Battle of Britain.

And now, it seemed, she was married to the black sheep of the Fortescue family, for Neele assumed that the disagreement with his father, referred to primly by Miss Griffith, stood for some disgraceful incident in young Lancelot Fortescue's career.

Lancelot Fortescue! What a name! And what was the other son—Percival? He wondered what the first Mrs. Fortescue had been like? She'd had a curious taste in Christian names . . .

He drew the phone towards him and dialed TOL. He asked for Baydon Heath 3400.

Presently a man's voice said, "Baydon Heath 3400."

"I want to speak to Mrs. Fortescue or Miss Fortescue."

"Sorry. They aren't in, either of 'em."

The voice struck Inspector Neele as slightly alcoholic.

"Are you the butler?"

"That's right."

"Mr. Fortescue has been taken seriously ill."

"I know. They rung up and said so. But there's nothing I can do about it. Mr. Val's away up North and

Mrs. Fortescue's out playing golf. Mrs. Val's gone to London but she'll be back for dinner and Miss Elaine's out with her Brownies."

"Is there no one in the house I can speak to about Mr. Fortescue's illness? It's important."

"Well—I don't know." The man sounded doubtful. "There's Miss Ramsbottom—but she don't ever speak over the phone. Or there's Miss Dove—she's what you might call the 'ousekeeper."

"I'll speak to Miss Dove, please."

"I'll try and get hold of her."

His retreating footsteps were audible through the phone. Inspector Neele heard no approaching footsteps but a minute or two later a woman's voice spoke.

"This is Miss Dove speaking."

The voice was low and well poised, with clear-cut enunciation. Inspector Neele formed a favorable picture of Miss Dove.

"I am sorry to have to tell you, Miss Dove, that Mr. Fortescue died in St. Jude's Hospital a short time ago. He was taken suddenly ill in his office. I am anxious to get in touch with his relatives—"

"Of course. I had no idea—" She broke off. Her voice had held no agitation, but it was shocked. She went on: "It is all most unfortunate. The person you really want to get in touch with is Mr. Percival Fortescue. He would be the one to see to all the necessary arrangements. You might be able to get in touch with him at the Midland in Manchester or possibly at the Grand in Leicester. Or you might try Shearer and Bonds of Leicester. I don't know their telephone number, I'm afraid, but I know they are a firm on whom he was going to call and they might be able to inform you where he would be likely to be today. Mrs. Fortescue will certainly be in to dinner and she may be in to tea. It will be a great shock to her. It must have been very sudden? Mr. Fortescue was quite well when he left here this morning."

"You saw him before he left?"

"Oh yes. What was it? Heart?"

"Did he suffer from heart trouble?"

"No—no—I don't think so—but I thought as it was so sudden—" She broke off. "Are you speaking from St. Jude's Hospital? Are you a doctor?"

"No, Miss Dove, I'm not a doctor. I'm speaking from Mr. Fortescue's office in the city. I am Detective Inspector Neele of the C.I.D. and I shall be coming down to see you as soon as I can get there."

"Detective Inspector? Do you mean—what do you mean?"

"It was a case of sudden death, Miss Dove, and when there is a sudden death we get called to the scene, especially when the deceased man hasn't seen a doctor lately, which I gather was the case?"

It was only the faintest suspicion of a question mark, but the young woman responded.

"I know. Percival made an appointment twice for him, but he wouldn't keep it. He was quite unreasonable —they've all been worried—"

She broke off and then resumed in her former assured manner.

"If Mrs. Fortescue returns to the house before you arrive, what do you want me to tell her?"

Practical as they make 'em, thought Inspector Neele.

Aloud he said, "Just tell her that in a case of sudden death we have to make a few inquiries. Routine inquiries."

He hung up.

Chapter Three

Neele pushed the telephone away and looked sharply at Miss Griffith.

"So they've been worried about him lately," he said. "Wanted him to see a doctor. You didn't tell me that."

"I didn't think of it," said Miss Griffith, and added, "He never seemed to me really ill——"

"Not ill—but what?"

"Well, just odd. Unlike himself. Peculiar in his manner."

"Worried about something?"

"Oh no, not worried. It's we who were worried."

Inspector Neele waited patiently.

"It's difficult to say, really," said Miss Griffith. "He had moods, you know. Sometimes he was quite boisterous. Once or twice, frankly, I thought he had been drinking. . . . He boasted and told the most extraordinary stories which I'm sure couldn't possibly have been true. For most of the time I've been here he was always very close about his affairs—not giving anything away, you know. But lately he's been quite different, expansive, and positively—well, flinging money about. Most unlike his usual manner. Why, when the office boy had to go to his grandmother's funeral, Mr. Fortescue called him in and gave him a five-pound note and told him to put it on the second favorite and then roared with laughter. He wasn't—well, he just wasn't like himself. That's all I can say."

"As though, perhaps, he had something on his mind?"

"Not in the usual meaning of the term. It was as though he were looking forward to something pleasurable—exciting."

"Possibly a big deal that he was going to pull off?"

Miss Griffith agreed with more conviction. "Yes—yes, that's much more what I mean. As though everyday things didn't matter any more. He was excited. And some very odd-looking people came to see him on business. People who'd never been here before. It worried Mr. Percival dreadfully."

"Oh, it worried him, did it?"

"Yes. Mr. Percival's always been very much in his father's confidence, you see. His father relied on him. But lately—"

"Lately they weren't getting along so well?"

"Well, Mr. Fortescue was doing a lot of things that Mr. Percival thought unwise. Mr. Percival is always very careful and prudent. But suddenly his father didn't listen to him any more, and Mr. Percival was very upset."

"And they had a real row about it all?"

Inspector Neele was still probing.

"I don't know about a row. . . . Of course, I realize

now Mr. Fortescue can't have been himself—shouting like that."

"Shouted, did he? What did he say?"

"He came right out in the typists' room—"

"So that you all heard?"

"Well—yes."

"And he called Percival names—abused him—swore at him . . . ? What did he say Percival had done?"

"It was more that he hadn't done anything . . . he called him a miserable, pettifogging little clerk. He said he had no large outlook, no conception of doing business in a big way. He said, 'I shall get Lance home again. He's worth ten of you—and he's married well. Lance has got guts even if he did risk a criminal prosecution once—' Oh dear, I oughtn't to have said that!" Miss Griffith, carried away as others before her had been under Inspector Neele's expert handling, was suddenly overcome with confusion.

"Don't worry," said Inspector Neele comfortingly. "What's past is past."

"Oh yes, it was a long time ago. Mr. Lance was just young and high-spirited and didn't really realize what he was doing."

Inspector Neele had heard that view before and didn't agree with it. But he passed on to fresh questions.

"Tell me a little more about the staff here."

Miss Griffith, hurrying to get away from her indiscretion, poured out information about the various personalities in the firm. Inspector Neele thanked her and then said he would like to see Miss Grosvenor again.

Detective Constable Waite sharpened his pencil. He remarked wistfully that this was a Ritzy joint. His glance wandered appreciatively over the huge chairs, the big desk and the indirect lighting.

"All these people have got Ritzy names, too," he

said. "Grosvenor—that's something to do with a duke. And Fortescue—that's a classy name, too."

Inspector Neele smiled.

"His father's name wasn't Fortescue. Fontescu—and he came from somewhere in central Europe. I suppose this man thought Fortescue sounded better."

Detective Constable Waite looked at his superior officer with awe.

"So you know all about him?"

"I just looked up a few things before coming along on the call."

"Not got a record, had he?"

"Oh no. Mr. Fortescue was much too clever for that. He's had certain connections with the Black Market and put through one or two deals that are questionable, to say the least of it, but they've always been just within the law."

"I see," said Waite. "Not a nice man."

"A twister," said Neele. "But we've got nothing on him. The Inland Revenue have been after him for a long time, but he's been too clever for them. Quite a financial genius, the late Mr. Fortescue."

"The sort of man," said Constable Waite, "who might have enemies?" He spoke hopefully.

"Oh yes, certainly enemies. But he was poisoned at home, remember. Or so it would seem. You know, Waite, I see a kind of pattern emerging. An old-fashioned, familiar kind of pattern. The good boy, Percival. The bad boy, Lance—attractive to women. The wife who's younger than her husband and who's vague about which course she's going to play golf on. It's all very, very familiar. But there's one thing that sticks out in a most incongruous way."

Constable Waite asked "What's that?" just as the door opened and Miss Grosvenor, her poise restored, and once more her glamorous self, inquired haughtily,

"You wished to see me?"

"I wanted to ask you a few questions about your employer—your late employer, perhaps I should say."

"Poor soul," said Miss Grosvenor unconvincingly.

"I want to know if you have noticed any difference in him lately."

"Well, yes. I did, as a matter of fact."

"In what way?"

"I couldn't really say. . . . He seemed to talk a lot of nonsense. I couldn't really believe half of what he said. And then he lost his temper very easily, especially with Mr. Percival. Not with me, because of course I never argue. I just say, 'Yes, Mr. Fortescue,' whatever peculiar thing he says—said, I mean."

"Did he ever—well, make any passes at you?"

Miss Grosvenor replied rather regretfully, "Well, no, I couldn't exactly say that."

"There's just one other thing, Miss Grosvenor. Was Mr. Fortescue in the habit of carrying grain about in his pocket?"

Miss Grosvenor displayed a lively surprise.

"Grain? In his pocket? Do you mean, to feed pigeons or something?"

"It could have been for that purpose."

"Oh, I'm sure he didn't. Mr. Fortescue? Feed pigeons? Oh no."

"Could he have had barley—or rye—in his pocket today for any special reason? A sample, perhaps? Some deal in grain?"

"Oh no. He was expecting the Asiatic Oil people this afternoon. And the President of the Atticus Building Society. . . . No one else."

"Oh well—" Neele dismissed the subject and Miss Grosvenor with a wave of the hand.

"Lovely legs she's got," said Constable Waite with a sigh. "And super nylons——"

"Legs are no help to me," said Inspector Neele. "I'm left with what I had before. A pocket full of rye—and no explanation of it."

Chapter Four

Mary Dove paused on her way downstairs and looked out through the big window on the stairs. A car had just driven up from which two men were alighting. The taller of the two stood for a moment with his back to the house surveying his surroundings. Mary Dove appraised the two men thoughtfully. Inspector Neele and presumably a subordinate.

She turned from the window and looked at herself in the full-length mirror that hung on the wall where the staircase turned. . . . She saw a small, demure figure with immaculate white collar and cuffs on a beige gray dress. Her dark hair was parted in the middle and drawn back in two shining waves to a knot in the back of her neck. . . . The lipstick she used was a pale rose color.

On the whole, Mary Dove was satisfied with her appearance. A very faint smile on her lips, she went on down the stairs.

Inspector Neele, surveying the house, was saying to himself:

Call it a lodge, indeed! Yewtree Lodge! The affectation of these rich people! The house was what he, Inspector Neele, would call a mansion. He knew what a lodge was. He'd been brought up in one. The lodge at the gates of Hartington Park, that vast, unwieldy Palladian house with its twenty-nine bedrooms which had now been taken over by the National Trust. The lodge had been small and attractive from the outside, and had been damp, uncomfortable and devoid of anything but the most primitive form of sanitation within. Fortunately these facts had been accepted as quite proper and fitting by Inspector Neele's parents. They had no rent to pay and nothing whatever to do except open and shut the gates when required, and there were always plenty of rabbits and an occasional pheasant or so for the pot. Mrs. Neele had never discovered the pleasures of electric irons, slow combustion stoves, airing cupboards, hot and cold water from taps, and the switching on of light by a mere flick of a finger. In winter the Neeles had an oil lamp, and in summer they went to bed when it got dark. They were a healthy family and a happy one, all thoroughly behind the times.

So when Inspector Neele heard the word Lodge, it was his childhood memories that stirred. But this place, this pretentiously named Yewtree Lodge was just the kind of mansion that rich people built themselves and then called it their "little place in the country." It wasn't in the country either, according to Inspector Neele's idea of the country. The house was a large, solid, red brick structure, sprawling lengthwise rather than upward, with rather too many gables, and a vast number of leaded paned windows. The gardens were highly artificial—all laid out in rose beds and pergolas and pools, and living up to the name of the house with large numbers of clipped yew hedges.

Plenty of yew here for anybody with a desire to obtain the raw material of taxine. Over on the right, behind the rose pergola, there was a bit of actual Nature left—a vast yew tree of the kind one associates with churchyards, its branches held up by stakes, like a kind of Moses of the forest world. That tree, the Inspector thought, had been there long before the rash of newly-built red brick houses had begun to spread over the countryside. It had been there before the golf courses had been laid out and the fashionable architects had walked round with their rich clients pointing out the advantages of the various sites. And since it was a valuable antique, the tree had been kept and incorporated in the new setup and had, perhaps, given its name to the new, desirable residence. Yewtree Lodge. And possibly the berries from that very tree—

Inspector Neele cut off these unprofitable speculations. Must get on with the job. He rang the bell.

It was opened promptly by a middle-aged man who fitted in quite accurately with the mental image Inspector Neele had formed of him over the phone. A man with a rather spurious air of smartness, a shifty eye and a rather unsteady hand.

Inspector Neele announced himself and his subordinate and had the pleasure of seeing an instant look of alarm come into the butler's eye. Neele did not attach too much importance to that. It might easily have nothing to do with the death of Rex Fortescue. It was quite possibly a purely automatic reaction.

"Has Mrs. Fortescue returned yet?"

"No, sir."

"Nor Mr. Percival Fortescue? Nor Miss Fortescue?"

"No, sir."

"Then I would like to see Miss Dove, please."

The man turned his head slightly. "Here's Miss Dove now—coming downstairs."

Inspector Neele took in Miss Dove as she came composedly down the wide staircase. This time the mental picture did not correspond with the reality. Unconsciously the word housekeeper had conjured up a vague impression of someone large and authoritative, dressed in black, with somewhere concealed about her a jingle of keys.

The Inspector was quite unprepared for the small, trim figure descending towards him. The soft dove-colored tones of her dress, the white collar and cuffs, the neat waves of hair, the faint Mona Lisa smile. It all seemed, somehow, just a little unreal, as though this young woman of under thirty was playing a part: not, he thought, the part of a housekeeper, but the part of Mary Dove. Her appearance was directed towards living up to her name.

She greeted him composedly. "Inspector Neele?"

"Yes. This is Sergeant Hay. Mr. Fortescue, as I told you through the phone, died in St. Jude's Hospital at 12:43. It seems likely that his death was the result of something he ate at breakfast this morning. I should be glad therefore if Sergeant Hay could be taken to the kitchen where he can make inquiries as to the food served."

Her eyes met his for a moment, thoughtfully; then she nodded.

"Of course," she said. She turned to the uneasily hovering butler. "Crump, will you take Sergeant Hay out and show him whatever he wants to see."

The two men departed together. Mary Dove said to Neele, "Will you come in here?"

She opened the door of a room and preceded him into it. It was a characteristic apartment, clearly labeled "Smoking Room," with paneling, rich upholstery, large stuffed chairs, and a suitable set of sporting prints on the walls.

"Please sit down."

He sat and Mary Dove sat opposite him. She chose, he noticed, to face the light. An unusual preference for a woman. Still more unusual if a woman had anything to hide. But perhaps Mary Dove had nothing to hide.

"It is very unfortunate," she said, "that none of the family is available. Mrs. Fortescue may return at any minute. And so may Mrs. Val. I have sent wires to Mr. Percival Fortescue at various places."

"Thank you, Miss Dove."

"You say that Mr. Fortescue's death was caused by something he may have eaten for breakfast? Food poisoning, you mean?"

"Possibly." He watched her.

She said composedly, "It seems unlikely. For breakfast this morning there were bacon and scrambled eggs, coffee, toast and marmalade. There was also a cold ham on the sideboard, but that had been cut yesterday, and no one felt any ill effects. No fish of any kind was served, no sausages—nothing like that."

"I see you know exactly what was served."

"Naturally. I order the meals. For dinner last night—"

"No." Inspector Neele interrupted her. "It would not be a question of dinner last night."

"I thought the onset of food poisoning could sometimes be delayed as much as twenty-four hours."

"Not in this case. . . . Will you tell me exactly what Mr. Fortescue ate and drank before leaving the house this morning?"

"He had early tea brought to his room at eight o'clock. Breakfast was at a quarter past nine. Mr. Fortescue, as I have told you, had scrambled eggs, bacon, coffee, toast and marmalade."

"Any cereal?"

"No, he doesn't like cereals."

"The sugar for the coffee—is it lump sugar or granulated?"

"Lump. But Mr. Fortescue does not take sugar in his coffee."

"Is he in the habit of taking any medicines in the morning? Salts? A tonic? Some digestive remedy?"

"No, nothing of that kind."

"Did you have breakfast with him also?"

"No. I do not take meals with the family."

"Who was at breakfast?"

"Mrs. Fortescue. Miss Fortescue. Mrs. Val Fortescue. Mr. Percival Fortescue, of course, was away."

"And Mrs. and Miss Fortescue ate the same things for breakfast?"

"Mrs. Fortescue has only coffee, orange juice and toast. Mrs. Val and Miss Fortescue always eat a hearty breakfast. Beisdes eating scrambled eggs and cold ham, they would probably have a cereal as well. Mrs. Val drinks tea, not coffee."

Inspector Neele reflected for a moment. The opportunities seemed at least to be narrowing down. Three people, and three people only, had had breakfast with the deceased: his wife, his daughter and his daughter-in-law. Either of them might have seized an opportunity to add taxine to his cup of coffee. The bitterness of the coffee would have masked the bitter taste of the taxine. There was the early morning tea, of course, but Bernsdorff had intimated that the taste would be noticeable in tea. But perhaps, first thing in the morning, before the senses were alert. . . . He looked up to find Mary Dove watching him.

"Your questions about tonic and medicines seem to me rather odd, Inspector," she said. "It seems to imply that either there was something wrong with a medicine, or that something had been added to it. Surely neither of those processes could be described as food poisoning."

Neele eyed her steadily.

"I did not say, definitely, that Mr. Fortescue died of food poisoning. But—some kind of poisoning. In fact, just poisoning."

She repeated softly, "Poisoning. . . ."

She appeared neither startled nor dismayed, merely interested. Her attitude was of one sampling a new experience.

In fact, she said as much, remarking after a moment's reflection: "I have never had anything to do with a poisoning case before."

"It's not very pleasant," Neele informed her dryly.

"No, I suppose not. . . ."

She thought about it for a moment and then looked up at him with a sudden smile.

"I didn't do it," she said. "But I suppose everybody will tell you that!"

"Have you any idea who did do it, Miss Dove?"

She shrugged her shoulders. "Frankly, he was an odious man. Anybody might have done it."

"But people aren't poisoned just for being 'odious,' Miss Dove. There usually has to be a pretty solid motive."

"Yes, of course."

She was thoughtful.

"Do you care to tell me something about the household here?"

She looked up at him. He was a little startled to find her eyes cool and amused.

"This isn't exactly a statement you're asking me to make, is it? No, it couldn't be, because your Sergeant is busy upsetting the domestic staff. I shouldn't like to have what I say read out in court, but all the same I should rather like to say it—unofficially. Off the record, so to speak?"

"Go ahead then, Miss Dove. I've no witness, as you've already observed."

She leaned back, swinging one slim foot and narrowing her eyes.

"Let me start by saying that I've no feeling of loyalty to my employers. I work for them because it's a job that pays well and I insist that it should pay well."

"I was a little surprised to find you doing this type of job. It struck me that with your brains and education—"

"I ought to be confined in an office? Or compiling files in a Ministry? My dear Inspector Neele, this is the perfect racket. People will pay anything—anything—to be spared domestic worries. To find and engage a staff is a thoroughly tedious job. Writing to agencies, putting in advertisements, interviewing people, making arrangements for interviews, and finally keeping the whole thing running smoothly—it takes a certain capacity which most of these people haven't got."

"And suppose your staff, when you've assembled it, runs out on you? I've heard of such things."

Mary smiled. "If necessary, I can make the beds, dust the rooms, cook a meal and serve it without anyone noticing the difference. Of course, I don't advertise that fact. It might give rise to ideas. But I can always be sure of tiding over any little gap. But there aren't often gaps. I work only for the extremely rich who will pay anything to be comfortable. I pay top prices and so I get the best of what's going."

"Such as the butler?"

She threw him an amused, appreciative glance.

"There's always that trouble with a couple. Crump stays because of Mrs. Crump, who is one of the best cooks I've ever come across. She's a jewel, and one would put up with a good deal to keep her. Our Mr.

Fortescue likes his food—liked, I should say. In this household nobody has any scruples and they have plenty of money. Butter, eggs, cream, Mrs. Crump can command what she likes. As for Crump, he just makes the grade. His silver's all right, and his waiting at table is not too bad. I keep the key of the wine cellar and a sharp eye on the whiskey and gin, and supervise his valeting."

Inspector Neele raised his eyebrows.

"The admirable Miss Crichton."

"I find one must know how to do everything oneself. Then—one need never do it. But you wanted to know my impression of the family."

"If you don't mind."

"They are really all quite odious. The late Mr. Fortescue was the kind of crook who is always careful to play safe. He boasted a great deal of his various smart dealings. He was rude and over-bearing in manner and was a definite bully. Mrs. Fortescue—Adele—is his second wife and about thirty years younger than he is. He came across her at Brighton. She was a manicurist on the lookout for big money. She is very good-looking —a real sexy piece, if you know what I mean."

Inspector Neele was shocked but managed not to show it. A girl like Mary Dove ought not to say such things, he felt.

The young lady was continuing composedly:

"Adele married him for his money, of course, and his son, Percival, and his daughter, Elaine, were simply livid about it. They're as nasty as they can be to her, but very wisely she doesn't care or even notice. She knows she's got the old man where she wants him. Oh dear, the wrong tense again. I haven't really grasped yet that he's dead. . . ."

"Let's hear about the son."

"Dear Percival? Val, as his wife calls him. Percival

is a mealy-mouthed hypocrite. He's prim and sly and cunning. He's terrified of his father and has always let himself be bullied, but he's quite clever at getting his own way. Unlike his father, he's mean about money. Economy is one of his passions. That's why he's been so long about finding a house of his own. Having a suite of rooms here saved his pocket."

"And his wife?"

"Jennifer's meek and seems very stupid. But I'm not so sure. She was a hospital nurse before her marriage— nursed Percival through pneumonia to a romantic conclusion. The old man was disappointed by the marriage. He's a snob and wanted Percival to make what he called a 'good marriage.' He despises poor Mrs. Val and snubs her. She dislikes—disliked him a good deal, I think. Her principal interests are shopping and the cinema; her principal grievance is that her husband keeps her short of money."

"What about the daughter?"

"Elaine? I'm rather sorry for Elaine. She's not a bad sort. One of those great schoolgirls who never grow up. She plays games quite well, and runs Girl Guides and Brownies and all that sort of thing. There was some sort of affair not long ago with a disgruntled young schoolmaster, but Father discovered the young man had communistic ideas and came down on the romance like a ton of bricks."

"She hadn't got the spirit to stand up to him?"

"*She* had. It was the young man who ratted. A question of money yet again, I fancy. Elaine is not particularly attractive, poor dear."

"And the other son?"

"I've never seen him. He's attractive, by all accounts, and a thoroughly bad lot. Some little matter of a forged check in the past. He lives in East Africa."

"And is estranged from his father."

"Yes, Mr. Fortescue couldn't cut him off with a shilling because he'd already made him a junior partner in the firm, but he's held no communication with him for years, and in fact if Lance was ever mentioned, he used to say, 'Don't talk to me of that rascal. He's no son of mine.' All the same—"

"Yes, Miss Dove?"

Mary said slowly, "All the same, I shouldn't be surprised if old Fortescue hadn't been planning to get him back here."

"What makes you think that?"

"Because, about a month ago, old Fortescue had a terrific row with Percival—he found out something that Percival had been doing behind his back—I don't know what it was—and he was absolutely furious. Percival suddenly stopped being the white-headed boy. He's been quite different lately, too."

"Mr. Fortescue was quite different?"

"'No. I meant Percival. He's gone about looking worried to death."

"Now, what about servants? You've already described the Crumps. Who else is there?"

"Gladys Martin is the parlormaid or waitress, as they like to call themselves nowadays. She does the downstairs rooms, lays the tables, clears away and helps Crump wait at table. Quite a decent sort of girl, but very nearly half-witted. The adenoidal type."

Neele nodded.

"The housemaid is Ellen Curtis. Elderly, very crabbed, and very cross, but has been in good service and is a first-class housemaid. The rest is outside help —odd women who come in."

"And those are the only people living here?"

"There's old Miss Ramsbottom."

"Who is she?"

"Mr. Fortescue's sister-in-law—his first wife's sister.

His wife was a good deal older than he was and her sister again is a good deal older than she—which makes her well over seventy. She has a room of her own on the second floor—does her own cooking and all that, with just a woman coming in to clean. She's rather eccentric and she never liked her brother-in-law, but she came here while her sister was alive and stayed on when she died. Mr. Fortescue never bothered about her much. She's quite a character, though, is Aunt Effie."

"And that is all."

"That's all."

"So we come to you, Miss Dove."

"You want particulars? I'm an orphan. I took a secretarial course at the St. Alfred's Secretarial College. I took a job as shorthand typist, left it and took another, decided I was in the wrong racket, and started on my present career. I have been with three different employers. After about a year or eighteen months, I get tired of a particular place and move on. I have been at Yew-tree Lodge just over a year. I will type out the names and addresses of my various employers and give them, with a copy of my references, to Sergeant—Hay, is it? Will that be satisfactory?"

"Perfectly, Miss Dove." Neele was silent for a moment, enjoying a mental image of Miss Dove tampering with Mr. Fortescue's breakfast. His mind went back further, and he saw her methodically gathering yew berries in a little basket. With a sigh he returned to the present and reality. "Now, I would like to see the girl—er, Gladys—and then the housemaid, Ellen." He added as he rose, "By the way, Miss Dove, can you give me any idea why Mr. Fortescue would be carrying loose grain in his pocket?"

"Grain?" She stared at him with what appeared to be genuine surprise.

"Yes, grain. Does that suggest something to you, Miss Dove?"

"Nothing at all."

"Who looked after his clothes?"

"Crump."

"I see. Did Mr. Fortescue and Mrs. Fortescue occupy the same bedroom?"

"Yes. He had a dressing room and bath, of course, and so did she. . . ." Mary glanced down at her wrist watch. "I really think that she ought to be back very soon now."

The Inspector had risen. He said in a pleasant voice:

"Do you know one thing, Miss Dove? It strikes me as very odd that even though there are three golf courses in the immediate neighborhood, it has yet not been possible to find Mrs. Fortescue on one of them before now?"

"It would not be so odd, Inspector, if she did not actually happen to be playing golf at all."

Mary's voice was dry. The Inspector said sharply:

"I was distinctly informed that she was playing golf."

"She took her golf clubs and announced her intention of doing so. She was driving her own car, of course."

He looked at her steadily, perceiving the inference.

"Whom was she playing with? Do you know?"

"I think it possible that it might be Mr. Vivian Dubois."

Neele contented himself by saying, "I see."

"I'll send Gladys in to you. She'll probably be scared to death." Mary paused for a moment by the door, then she said:

"I should hardly advise you to go too much by all I've told you. I'm a malicious creature."

She went out. Inspector Neele looked at the closed door and wondered. Whether actuated by malice or not, what she had told him could not fail to be suggestive.

If Rex Fortescue had been deliberately poisoned, and it seemed almost certain that that was the case, then the setup at Yewtree Lodge seemed highly promising. Motives appeared to be lying thick on the ground.

Chapter Five

The girl who entered the room with obvious unwilling-
ness was an unattractive, frightened-looking girl, who
managed to look sluttish in spite of being tall and
smartly dressed in a claret-colored uniform.

She said at once, fixing imploring eyes upon him:

"I didn't do anything. I didn't really. I don't know
anything about it."

"That's all right," said Neele heartily. His voice had
changed slightly. It sounded more cheerful and a good
deal commoner in intonation. He wanted to put the
frightened rabbit, Gladys, at her ease.

"Sit down here," he went on. "I just want to know
about breakfast this morning."

"I didn't do anything at all."

"Well, you laid the breakfast, didn't you?"

"Yes, I did that." Even that admission came unwillingly. She looked both guilty and terrified, but Inspector
Neele was used to witnesses who looked like that. He

went on cheerfully, trying to put her at her ease, asking questions: Who had come down first? And who next?

Elaine Fortescue had been the first down to breakfast. She'd come in just as Crump was bringing in the coffeepot. Mrs. Fortescue was down next, and then Mrs. Val, and the master last. They waited on themselves. The tea and coffee and the hot dishes were all on hot plates on the sideboard.

He learnt little of importance from her that he did not know already. The food and drink were as Mary Dove had described them. The master and Mrs. Fortescue and Miss Elaine took coffee and Mrs. Val took tea. Everything had been quite as usual.

Neele questioned her about herself and here she answered more readily. She'd been in the NAAFI, a sort of USO called Navy, Army, and Air Forces Institute, and after that in a café at Eastbourne. Then she thought she'd like to try private service and had come to Yewtree Lodge last September. She'd been there two months.

"And you like it?"

"Well, it's all right, I suppose." She added, "It's not so hard on your feet, but you don't get so much freedom. . . ."

"Tell me about Mr. Fortescue's clothes—his suits. Who looked after them? Brushed them and all that?"

Gladys looked faintly resentful. "Mr. Crump's supposed to. But half the time he makes me do it."

"Who brushed and pressed the suit Mr. Fortescue had on today?"

"I don't remember which one he wore. He's got ever so many."

"Have you ever found grain in the pocket of one of his suits?"

"Grain?" She looked puzzled.

"Rye, to be exact."

"Rye? That's bread, isn't it? A sort of black bread—got a nasty taste, I always think."

"That's bread made from rye. Rye is the grain itself. There was some found in the pocket of your master's coat."

"In his coat pocket?"

"Yes. Do you know how it got there?"

"Couldn't say, I'm sure. I never saw any."

He could get no more from her. For a moment or two he wondered if she knew more about the matter than she was willing to admit. She certainly seemed embarrassed and on the defensive, but on the whole he put it down to a natural fear of the police.

When he finally dismissed her, she asked:

"It's really true, is it? He's dead?"

"Yes, he's dead."

"Very sudden, wasn't it? They said when they rang up from the office that he'd had a kind of fit."

"Yes—it was a kind of fit."

Gladys said, "A girl I used to know had fits. Come on any time, they did. Used to scare me."

For the moment this reminiscence seemed to overcome her suspicions.

Inspector Neele made his way to the kitchen.

His reception was immediate and alarming. A woman of vast proportions, with a red face and armed with a rolling pin, stepped towards him in a menacing fashion.

"Police, indeed," she said. "Coming here and saying my cooking's poisoned the master. Nothing of the kind, I'd have you know. Anything I've sent in to the dining-room has been just what it should be. Coming here and saying I poisoned the master. I'll have the law on you, police or no police. No bad food's ever been served in this house."

It was some time before Inspector Neele could appease the irate artist. Sergeant Hay looked in grinning from the pantry, and Inspector Neele gathered that he had already run the gantlet of Mrs. Crump's wrath.

The scene was terminated by the ringing of the telephone.

Neele went out into the hall to find Mary Dove taking the call. She was writing down a message on a pad. Turning her head over her shoulder, she said, "It's a telegram."

The call concluded, she replaced the receiver and handed the pad on which she had been writing to the Inspector. The place of origin was Paris and the message ran as follows:

Fortescue Yewtree Lodge Baydon Heath Surrey. Sorry your letter delayed. Will be with you tomorrow about teatime. Shall expect roast veal for dinner. Lance.

Inspector Neele raised his eyebrows.

"So the Prodigal Son had been summoned home," he said.

Chapter Six

At the moment when Rex Fortescue had been drinking his last cup of tea, Lance Fortescue and his wife had been sitting under the trees on the Champs Elysées watching the people walking past.

"It's all very well to say 'describe him,' Pat. I'm a rotten hand at descriptions. What do you want to know? The Guvnor's a bit of an old crook, you know. But you won't mind that? You must be used to that more or less."

"Oh yes," said Pat. "Yes, as you say, I'm acclimatized."

She tried to keep a certain forlornness out of her voice. Perhaps, she reflected, the whole world was really crooked, or was it just that she herself had been unfortunate?

She was a tall, long-legged girl, not beautiful but with a charm that was made up of vitality and a warm-hearted personality. She moved well, and had lovely, gleaming chestnut-brown hair. Perhaps, from a long association with horses, she had acquired the look of a thoroughbred filly.

Crookedness in the racing world she knew about. Now, it seemed she was to encounter crookedness in the financial world. Though for all that, it seemed that her father-in-law, whom she had not yet met, was, as far as the law was concerned, a pillar of rectitude. All these people who went about boasting of "smart work" were the same: technically they always managed to be within the law. Yet it seemed to her that her Lance, whom she loved, and who had admittedly strayed outside the ringed fence in earlier days, had an honesty that these successful practitioners of the crooked lacked.

"I don't mean," said Lance, "that he's a swindler, not anything like that. But he knows how to put over a fast one."

"Sometimes," said Pat, "I feel I hate people who put over fast ones." She added, "You're fond of him." It was a statement, not a question.

Lance considered it for a moment, and then said in a surprised kind of voice:

"Do you know, darling, I believe I am."

Pat laughed. He turned his head to look at her. His eyes narrowed. What a darling she was! He loved her. The whole thing was worth it for her sake.

"In a way, you know," he said, "it's hell going back. City life. Home on the 5:18. It's not my kind of life. I'm far more at home among the down-and-outs. But one's got to settle down sometime, I suppose. And with you to hold my hand, the process may even be quite a pleasant one. And since the old boy has come round, one ought to take advantage of it. I must say I was surprised when I got his letter. . . . Percival, of all people, blotting his copybook. Percival, the good little boy. Mind you, Percy was always sly. Yes, he was always sly."

"I don't think," said Patricia Fortescue, "that I'm going to like your brother Percival."

"Don't let me put you against him. Percy and I never got on—that's all there is to it. I blew my pocket money, he saved his. I had disreputable but entertaining friends, Percy made what's called 'worthwhile contacts.' Poles apart we were, he and I. I always thought him a poor fish, and he—sometimes, you know, I think he almost hated me. I don't know why, exactly. . . ."

"I think I can see why."

"Can you, darling? You're so brainy. You know, I've always wondered—it's a fantastic thing to say—but—"

"Well? Say it."

"I've wondered if it wasn't Percival who was behind that check business—you know, when the old man kicked me out—and was mad that he'd given me a share in the firm and so couldn't disinherit me! Because the queer thing was that I never forged that check—though of course nobody would believe that after that time I swiped funds out of the till and put it on a horse. I was dead sure I could put it back, and anyway it was my own cash, in a manner of speaking. But that check business—no. I don't know why I've got the ridiculous idea that Percival did that, but I have, somehow."

"But it wouldn't have done him any good. It was paid into your account."

"I know. So it doesn't make sense, does it?"

Pat turned sharply towards him. "You mean, he did it to get you chucked out of the firm?"

"I wondered. Oh well, it's a rotten thing to say. Forget it. I wonder what old Percy will say when he sees the Prodigal returned. Those pale, boiled-gooseberry eyes of his will pop right out of his head!"

"Does he know you are coming?"

"I shouldn't be surprised if he didn't know a damned thing! The old man's got rather a funny sense of humor, you know."

"But what has your brother done to upset your father so much?"

"That's what I'd like to know. Something must have made the old man livid. Writing off to me the way he did."

"When was it you got his first letter?"

"Must be four—no, five months ago. A cagey letter, but a distinct holding out of the olive branch. 'Your elder brother has proved himself unsatisfactory in many ways.' 'You seem to have sown your wild oats and settled down.' 'I can promise you that it will be well worth your while financially.' 'Shall welcome you and your wife.' You know, darling, I think my marrying you had a lot to do with it. The old boy was impressed that I'd married into a class above me."

Pat laughed.

"What? Into the aristocratic riffraff?"

He grinned. "That's right. But riffraff didn't register and aristocracy did. You should see Percival's wife. She's the kind who says 'Pass the preserves, please' and talks about a postage stamp."

Pat did not laugh. She was considering the women of the family into which she had married. It was a point of view which Lance had not taken into account.

"And your sister?" she asked.

"Elaine? Oh, she's all right. She was pretty young when I left home. Sort of an earnest girl, but probably she's grown out of that. Very intense over things."

It did not sound very reassuring. Pat said, "She never wrote to you—after you went away?"

"I didn't leave an address. But she wouldn't have, anyway. We're not a devoted family."

"No."

He shot a quick look at her.

"Got the windup? About my family? You needn't. We're not going to live with them, or anything like that. We'll have our own little place somewhere. Horses, dogs, anything you like."

"But there will still be the 5:18."

"For me, yes. To and fro to the city all togged up. But don't worry, sweet—there are rural pockets, even round London. And lately I've felt the sap of financial affairs rising in me. After all it's in my blood, from both sides of the family."

"You hardly remember your mother, do you?"

"She always seemed to me incredibly old. She was old, of course. Nearly fifty when Elaine was born. She wore lots of clinking things and lay on the sofa and used to read me stories about knights and ladies which bored me stiff. Tennyson's *Idylls of the King*. I suppose I was fond of her. . . . She was very—colorless, you know. I realize that, looking back."

"You don't seem to have been particularly fond of anybody," said Pat disapprovingly.

Lance grasped and squeezed her arm.

"I'm fond of you," he said.

Chapter Seven

Inspector Neele was still holding the telegraph message in his hand when he heard a car drive up to the front door and stop with a careless scrunching of brakes.

Mary Dove said, "That will be Mrs. Fortescue now."

Inspector Neele moved forwards to the front door. Out of the tail of his eye, he saw Mary Dove melt unobtrusively into the background and disappear. Clearly she intended to take no part in the forthcoming scene. A remarkable display of tact and discretion, and also a rather remarkable lack of curiosity. Most women, Inspector Neele decided, would have remained. . . .

As he reached the front door he was aware of the butler, Crump, coming forward from the back of the hall. So he had heard the car.

The car was a Rolls Bentley sports model coupé. Two people got out of it and came towards the house. As they reached the door, it opened. Surprised, Adele Fortescue stared at Inspector Neele.

He realized at once that she was a very beautiful woman, and he realized, too, the force of Mary Dove's comment which had so shocked him at the time. Adele Fortescue *was* a sexy piece. In figure and type she resembled the blonde Miss Grosvenor, but whereas Miss Grosvenor was all glamour without and all respectability within, Adele Fortescue was glamour all through. Her appeal was obvious, not subtle. It said simply to every man, "Here am I. I'm a woman." She spoke and moved and breathed sex, and yet, within it all, her eyes had a shrewd, appraising quality. Adele Fortescue, he thought, liked men, but she would always like money even better.

His eyes went on behind her to the figure who carried her golf clubs. He knew the type very well. It was the type that specialized in the young wives of rich and elderly men. Mr. Vivian Dubois, if this was he, had that rather forced masculinity which is, in reality, nothing of the kind. He was the type of man who "understands" women.

"Mrs. Fortescue?"

"Yes." It was a wide blue-eyed gaze. "But I don't know—"

"I am Inspector Neele. I'm afraid I have bad news for you."

"Do you mean—a burglary—something of that kind?"

"No, nothing of that kind. It is about your husband. He was taken seriously ill this morning."

"Rex? Ill?"

"We have been trying to get in touch with you since half past eleven this morning."

"Where is he? Here? Or in the hospital?"

"He was taken to St. Jude's Hospital. I'm afraid you must prepare yourself for a shock."

"You don't mean—he isn't—dead."

She lurched forward a little and clutched his arm. Gravely, feeling like someone playing a part in a stage performance, the Inspector supported her into the hall. Crump was hovering eagerly.

"Brandy she'll be needing," he said.

The deep voice of Mr. Dubois said, "That's right, Crump. Get the brandy." To the Inspector he said, "In here."

He opened a door on the left. The procession filed in. The Inspector and Adele Fortescue, Vivian Dubois, and Crump with a decanter and two glasses.

Adele Fortescue sank onto an easy chair, her eyes covered with her hand. She accepted the glass that the Inspector offered and took a tiny sip, then pushed it away.

"I don't want it," she said. "I'm all right. But tell me, what was it? A stroke, I suppose? Poor Rex."

"It wasn't a stroke, Mrs. Fortescue."

"Did you say you were an Inspector?" It was Mr. Dubois who made the inquiry.

Neele turned to him. "That's right," he said pleasantly. "Inspector Neele of the C.I.D."

He saw the alarm grow in the dark eyes. Mr. Dubois did not like the appearance of an Inspector of the C.I.D. He didn't like it at all.

"What's up?" he said. "Something wrong, eh?"

Quite unconsciously he backed away a little towards the door. Inspector Neele noted the movement.

"I'm afraid," he said to Mrs. Fortescue, "that there will have to be an inquest."

"An inquest? Do you mean—what *do* you mean?"

"I'm afraid this is all very distressing for you, Mrs. Fortescue." The words came smoothly. "It seemed advisable to find out as soon as possible exactly what Mr. Fortescue had to eat or drink before leaving for the office this morning."

"Do you mean he might have been poisoned?"

"Well, yes, it would seem so."

"I can't believe it. Oh, you mean food poisoning."
Her voice dropped half an octave on the last words.

His face wooden, his voice still smooth, Inspector
Neele said, "Why, yes, madam, what did you think I
meant?"

She ignored that question, hurrying on.

"But we've been all right—all of us."

"You can speak for all the members of the family?"

"Well, no—of course—I can't really."

Dubois said with a great show of consulting his
watch, "I'll have to push off. Adele. Dreadfully sorry.
You'll be all right, won't you? I mean, there are the
maids, and the little Dove and all that—"

"Oh, Vivian, don't. Don't go."

It was quite a wail, and it affected Mr. Dubois ad-
versely. His retreat quickened.

"Awfully sorry, old girl. Important engagement. I'm
putting up at the Dormy House, by the way, Inspector.
If you—er, want me for anything."

Inspector Neele nodded. He had no wish to detain
Mr. Dubois. But he recognized Mr. Dubois' departure
for what it was. Mr. Dubois was running away from
trouble.

Adele Fortescue said, in an attempt to carry off the
situation, "It's such a shock, to come back and find the
police in the house."

"I'm sure it must be. But you see, it was necessary to
act promptly in order to obtain the necessary specimens
of foodstuffs, coffee, tea, etc."

"Tea and coffee? But they're not poisonous? I expect
it's the awful bacon we sometimes get. It's quite un-
eatable sometimes."

"We shall find out, Mrs. Fortescue. Don't worry.
You'd be surprised at some of the things that can hap-

pen. We once had a case of digitalis poisoning. It turned out that foxglove leaves had been picked in mistake for horse-radish."

"You think something like that could happen here?"

"We shall know better after the autopsy, Mrs. Fortescue."

"The autop— Oh I see." She shivered.

The Inspector went on: "You've got a lot of yew round the house, haven't you, madam? There's no possibility, I suppose, of the berries or leaves having got— mixed up in anything?"

He was watching her closely. She stared at him.

"Yew berries? Are they poisonous?"

The wonder seemed a little too wide-eyed and innocent.

"Children have been known to eat them with unfortunate results."

Adele clasped her hands to her head.

"I can't bear to talk about it any more. Must I? I want to go and lie down. I can't stand any more. Mr. Percival Fortescue will arrange everything. I can't—I can't—it isn't fair to ask me."

"We are getting in touch with Mr. Percival Fortescue as soon as possible. Unfortunately he is away in the North of England."

"Oh yes, I forgot."

"There's just one other thing, Mrs. Fortescue. There was a small quantity of grain in your husband's pocket. Could you give me some explanation of that?"

She shook her head. She appeared quite bewildered.

"Would anyone have slipped it in there as a joke?"

"I don't see why it would be a joke."

Inspector Neele did not see either. He said, "I won't trouble you any further at present, Mrs. Fortescue. Shall I send one of the maids to you? Or Miss Dove?"

"What?" The word came abstractedly. He wondered what she had been thinking about.

She fumbled with her bag and pulled out a handkerchief. Her voice trembled.

"It's so awful," she said unsteadily. "I'm only just beginning to take it in. I've really been numbed up to now. Poor Rex. Poor dear Rex."

She sobbed in a manner that was almost convincing.

Inspector Neele watched her respectfully for a moment or two.

"It's been very sudden, I know," he said. "I'll send someone to you."

He went towards the door, opened it and passed through. He paused for a moment before looking into the room.

Adele Fortescue still held the handkerchief to her eyes. The ends of it hung down but did not quite obscure her mouth. On her lips was a very faint smile.

Chapter Eight

"I've got what I could, sir." So Sergeant Hay reported. "The marmalade, bit of the ham. Samples of tea, coffee and sugar, for what they're worth. Actual brews have been thrown out by now, of course, but there's one point. There was a good lot of coffee left over and they had it in the servants' hall at elevenses. That's important, I should say."

"Yes, that's important. Shows that if he took it in his coffee, it must have been slipped into the actual cup."

"By one of those present. Exactly. I've inquired, cautious like, about this yew stuff—berries or leaves— there's been none of it seen about the house. Nobody seems to know anything about the cereal in his pocket, either. . . . It just seems daft to them. Seems daft to me, too. He doesn't seem to have been one of those faddists who'll eat any mortal thing so long as it isn't cooked. My sister's husband's like that. Raw carrots, raw peas, raw turnips. But even he doesn't eat raw grain. Why, I should say it would swell up in your inside something awful."

The telephone rang, and on a nod from the Inspector Sergeant Hay sprinted off to answer it. Following him, Neele found that it was headquarters on the line. Contact had been made with Mr. Percival Fortescue, who was returning to London immediately.

As the Inspector replaced the telephone, a car drew up at the front door. Crump went to the door and opened it. The woman who stood there had her arms full of parcels. Crump took them from her.

"Thanks, Crump. Pay the taxi, will you? I'll have tea now. Is Mrs. Fortescue or Miss Elaine in?"

The butler hesitated, looking back over his shoulder.

"We've had bad news, ma'am," he said. "About the master."

"About Mr. Fortescue?"

Neele came forward. Crump said: "This is Mrs. Percival, sir."

"What is it? What's happened? An accident?"

The Inspector looked her over as he replied. Mrs. Percival Fortescue was a plump woman with a discontented mouth. Her age he judged to be about thirty. Her questions came with a kind of eagerness. The thought flashed across his mind that she must be very bored.

"I'm sorry to have to tell you that Mr. Fortescue was taken to St. Jude's Hospital this morning seriously ill and has since died."

"Died? You mean he's dead?" The news was clearly even more sensational than she had hoped for. "Dear me, this is a surprise. My husband's away. You'll have to get in touch with him. He's in the North somewhere. I daresay they'll know at the office. He'll have to see to everything. Things always happen at the most awkward moment, don't they?"

She paused for a moment, turning things over in her mind.

"It all depends, I suppose," she said, "where they'll have the funeral. Down here, I suppose. Or will it be in London?"

"That will be for the family to say."

"Of course. I only just wondered." For the first time she took direct cognizance of the man who was speaking to her.

"Are you from the office?" she asked. "You're not a doctor, are you?"

"I'm a police officer. Mr. Fortescue's death was very sudden and—"

She interrupted him.

"Do you mean he was murdered?"

It was the first time that word had been spoken. Neele carefully surveyed her eager, questioning face.

"Now why should you think that, madam?"

"Well, people are, sometimes. You said 'sudden.' And you're police. Have you seen her about it? What did she say?"

"I don't quite understand to whom you are referring?"

"Adele, of course. I always told Val his father was crazy to go marrying a woman years younger than himself. There's no fool like an old fool. Besotted about that awful creature, he was. And now look what comes of it. . . . A nice mess we're all in. Pictures in the paper and reporters coming round."

She paused, obviously visualizing the future in a series of crude, highly-colored pictures. He thought that the prospect was still not wholly unpleasing. She turned back to him.

"What was it? Arsenic?"

In a repressive voice Inspector Neele said, "The cause

of death has yet to be ascertained. There will be an autopsy and an inquest."

"But you know already, don't you? Or you wouldn't come down here."

There was a sudden shrewdness in her plump, rather foolish face.

"You've been asking about what he ate and drank, I suppose? Dinner last night. Breakfast this morning. And all the drinks, of course."

He could see her mind ranging vividly over all the possibilities. He said, with caution, "It seems possible that Mr. Fortescue's illness resulted from something he ate at breakfast."

"Breakfast?" She seemed surprised. "That's difficult. I don't see how . . ."

She paused and shook her head.

"I don't see how she could have done it then . . . unless she slipped something into the coffee when Elaine and I weren't looking . . ."

A quiet voice spoke softly beside them:

"Your tea is all ready in the library, Mrs. Val."

Mrs. Val jumped.

"Oh, thank you, Miss Dove. Yes, I could do with a cup of tea. Really, I feel quite bowled over. What about you, Mr.—Inspector—"

"Thank you, not just now."

The plump figure hesitated and then went slowly away.

As she disappeared through a doorway, Mary Dove murmured softly, "I don't think she's ever heard of the term slander."

Inspector Neele did not reply. Mary Dove went on: "Is there anything I can do for you?"

"Where can I find the housemaid, Ellen?"

"I will take you to her. She's just gone upstairs."

ii.

Ellen proved to be grim but unafraid. Her sour old face looked triumphantly at the Inspector.

"It's shocking business, sir. And I never thought I'd live to find myself in a house where that sort of thing has been going on. But in a way I can't say that it surprises me. I ought to have given my notice in long ago and that's a fact. I don't like the language that's used in this house, and I don't like the amount of drink that's taken, and I don't approve of the goings-on there've been. I've nothing against Mrs. Crump, but Crump and that girl Gladys just don't know what proper service is. But it's the goings-on that I mind about most."

"What goings-on do you mean exactly?"

"You'll soon hear about them if you don't know already. It's common talk all over the place. They've been seen here, there and everywhere. All this pretending to play golf—or tennis. And I've seen things with my own eyes in this house. The library door was open and there they were, kissing and canoodling."

The venom of the spinster was deadly. Neele really felt it unnecessary to say "Whom do you mean?" but he said it nevertheless.

"Who should I mean? The mistress—and that man. No shame about it, they hadn't. But if you ask me, the master had got wise to it. Put someone on to watch them, he had. Divorce, that's what it would have come to. Instead, it's come to *this*."

"When you say this, you mean—"

"You've been asking questions, sir, about what the master ate and drank and who gave it to him. They're in it together, sir, that's what I'd say. He got the stuff from somewhere, and she gave it to the master, that was the way of it, I've no doubt."

"Have you ever seen any yew berries in the house, or thrown away anywhere?"

The small eyes glinted curiously.

"Yew? Nasty, poisonous stuff. Never you touch those berries, my mother said to me when I was a child. Was that what was used, sir?"

"We don't know yet what was used."

"I've never seen her fiddling about with yew." Ellen sounded disappointed. "No, I can't say I've seen anything of that kind."

Neele questioned her about the grain found in Fortescue's pocket, but here again he drew a blank.

"No, sir. I know nothing about that."

He went on to further questions, but with no gainful result. Finally, he asked if he could see Miss Ramsbottom.

Ellen looked doubtful.

"I could ask her, but it's not everyone she'll see. She's a very old lady, you know, and she's a bit odd."

The Inspector pressed his demand, and rather unwillingly Ellen led him along a passage and up a short flight of stairs to what he thought had probably been designed as a nursery suite.

He glanced out of a passage window as he followed her and saw Sergeant Hay standing by the yew tree talking to a man who was evidently a gardener.

Ellen tapped on a door, and when she received an answer, opened it and said, "There's a police gentleman here who would like to speak to you, miss."

The answer was apparently in the affirmative, for she drew back and motioned Neele to go in.

The room he entered was almost fantastically overfurnished. The Inspector felt rather as though he had taken a step backward into not merely Edwardian but

Victorian times. At a table drawn up to a gas fire an old lady was sitting laying out a patience. She wore a maroon-colored dress and her sparse gray hair was slicked down each side of her face.

Without looking up or discontinuing her game, she said impatiently, "Well, come in, come in. Sit down if you like."

The invitation was not easy to accept as every chair appeared to be covered with tracts or publications of a religious nature.

As she moved them slightly aside on the sofa, Miss Ramsbottom asked sharply, "Interested in mission work?"

"Well, I'm afraid I'm not very, ma'am."

"Wrong. You should be. That's where the Christian spirit is nowadays. Darkest Africa. Had a young clergyman here last week. Black as your hat. But a true Christian."

Inspector Neele found it a little difficult to know what to say.

The old lady further disconcerted him by snapping, "I haven't got a wireless."

"I beg your pardon?"

"Oh, I thought perhaps you came about a wireless license. Or one of these silly forms. Well, man, what is it?"

"I'm sorry to have to tell you, Miss Ramsbottom, that your brother-in-law, Mr. Fortescue, was taken seriously ill and died this morning."

Miss Ramsbottom continued with her patience without any sign of perturbation, merely remarking in a conversational way, "Struck down at last in his arrogance and sinful pride. Well, it had to come."

"I hope it's not a shock to you?"

It obviously wasn't, but the Inspector wanted to hear what she would say.

Miss Ramsbottom gave him a sharp glance over the top of her spectacles and said, "If you mean I am not distressed, that is quite right. Rex Fortescue was always a sinful man and I never liked him."

"His death was very sudden—"

"As befits the ungodly," said the old lady with satisfaction.

"It seems possible that he may have been poisoned—"

The Inspector paused to observe the effect he had made.

He did not seem to have made any. Miss Ramsbottom merely murmured, "Red seven on black eight. Now I can move up the king."

Struck apparently by the Inspector's silence, she stopped with a card poised in her hand and said sharply, "Well, what did you expect me to say? I didn't poison him if that's what you want to know."

"Have you any idea who might have done so?"

"That's a very improper question," said the old lady sharply. "Living in this house are two of my dead sister's children. I decline to believe that anybody with Ramsbottom blood in them could be guilty of murder. Because it's murder you're meaning, isn't it?"

"I didn't say so, madam."

"Of course it's murder. Plenty of people have wanted to murder Rex in their time. A very unscrupulous man. And old sins have long shadows, as the saying goes."

"Have you anyone in particular in mind?"

Miss Ramsbottom swept up the cards and rose to her feet. She was a tall woman.

"I think you'd better go now," she said.

She spoke without anger, but with a kind of cold finality.

"If you want my opinion," she went on, "it was probably one of the servants. The butler looks to me a bit of a rascal, and that parlormaid is definitely subnormal. Good evening."

Inspector Neele found himself meekly walking out. Certainly a remarkable old lady. Nothing to be got out of her.

He came down the stairs into the square hall to find himself suddenly face to face with a tall, dark girl. She was wearing a damp mackintosh and she stared into his face with a curious blankness.

"I've just come back," she said. "And they told me—about Father—that he's dead."

"I'm afraid that's true."

She pushed out a hand behind her as though blindly seeking for support. She touched an oak chest and slowly, stiffly, she sat down on it.

"Oh no," she said. "No . . ."

Slowly two tears rolled down her cheeks.

"It's awful," she said. "I didn't think that I even liked him. . . . I thought I hated him. . . . But that can't be so, or I wouldn't mind. I do mind."

She sat there, staring in front of her, and again tears forced themselves from her eyes and down her cheeks.

Presently she spoke again, rather breathlessly.

"The awful thing is that it makes everything come right. I mean, Gerald and I can get married now. I can do everything that I want to do. But I hate it happening this way. I don't want Father to be dead. . . . Oh, I don't. Oh Daddy—Daddy . . ."

For the first time since he had come to Yewtree Lodge, Inspector Neele was startled by what seemed to be genuine grief for the dead man.

Chapter Nine

"Sounds like the wife to me," said the Assistant Commissioner. He had been listening attentively to Inspector Neele's report.

It had been an admirable précis of the case. Short, but with no relevant detail left out.

"Yes," said the A.C. "It looks like the wife. What do you think yourself, Neele, eh?"

Inspector Neele said that it looked like the wife to him, too. He reflected cynically that it usually was the wife—or the husband as the case might be.

"She had the opportunity all right. And motive?" The A.C. paused. "There is motive?"

"Oh, I think so, sir. This Mr. Dubois, you know."

"Think he was in it, too?"

"No, I shouldn't say that, sir." Inspector Neele weighed the idea. "A bit too fond of his own skin for that. He may have guessed what was in her mind, but I shouldn't imagine that he instigated it."

"No, too careful."

"Much too careful."

"Well, we mustn't jump to conclusions, but it seems a good working hypothesis. What about the other two who had opportunity?"

"That's the daughter and the daughter-in-law, sir. The daughter was mixed up with a young man whom her father didn't want her to marry. And he definitely wasn't marrying her unless she had the money. That gives her a motive. As to the daughter-in-law, I wouldn't like to say. Don't know enough about her yet. But any of the three of them could have poisoned him, and I don't see how anyone else could have done so. The parlormaid, the butler, the cook, they all handled the breakfast or brought it in, but I don't see how any of them could have been sure of Fortescue himself getting the taxine and nobody else. That is, if it was taxine."

The A.C. said, "It was taxine all right. I've just got the preliminary report."

"That settles that, then," said Inspector Neele. "We can go ahead."

"Servants seem all right?"

"The butler and the parlormaid both seem nervous. There's nothing uncommon about that. Often happens. The cook's fighting mad and the housemaid was grimly pleased. In fact, all quite natural and normal."

"There's nobody else whom you consider suspicious in any way?"

"No, I don't think so, sir." Involuntarily, Inspector Neele's mind went back to Mary Dove and her enigmatic smile. There had surely been a faint yet definite look of antagonism. Aloud, he said, "Now that we know it's taxine, there ought to be some evidence to be got as to how it was obtained or prepared."

"Just so. Well, go ahead, Neele. By the way, Mr. Percival Fortescue is here now. I've had a word or two with him and he's waiting to see you. We've located the other son, too. He's in Paris at the Bristol, leaving today. You'll have him met at the airport, I suppose."

"Yes, sir. That was my idea. . . ."

"Well, you'd better see Percival Fortescue now." The A.C. chuckled. "Percy Prim, that's what he is."

Mr. Percival Fortescue was a neat, fair man of thirty-odd with pale hair and eyelashes and a slightly pedantic way of speech.

"This has been a terrible shock to me, Inspector Neele, as you can well imagine."

"It must have been, Mr. Fortescue," said Inspector Neele.

"I can only say that my father was perfectly well when I left home the day before yesterday. This food poisoning, or whatever it was, must have been very sudden?"

"It was very sudden, yes. But it wasn't food poisoning, Mr. Fortescue."

Percival stared and frowned.

"No? So that's why—" he broke off.

"Your father," said Inspector Neele, "was poisoned by the administration of taxine."

"Taxine? I never heard of it."

"Very few people have, I should imagine. It is a poison that takes effect very suddenly and drastically."

The frown deepened.

"Are you telling me, Inspector, that my father was deliberately poisoned by someone?"

"It would seem so, yes, sir."

"That's terrible!"

"Yes indeed, Mr. Fortescue."

Percival murmured, "I understand now their attitude picions of who could— Really, I—" Again he broke off. After a pause he went on, "The funeral?" He spoke interrogatively.

"The inquest is fixed for tomorrow after the postmortem. The proceedings at the inquest will be purely formal and the inquest will be adjourned."

"I understand. That is usually the case?"

"Yes, sir. Nowadays."

"May I ask have you formed any ideas, any suspicions of who could— Really, I—" Again he broke off.

"It's rather early days for that, Mr. Fortescue," murmured Neele.

"Yes, I suppose so."

"All the same it would be helpful to us, Mr. Fortescue, if you could give us some idea of your father's testamentary dispositions. Or perhaps you could put me in touch with his solicitor."

"His solicitors are Billingsley, Horsethorpe & Walters of Bedford Square. As far as his will goes I think I can more or less tell you its main dispositions."

"If you will be kind enough to do so, Mr. Fortescue. It's a routine that has to be gone through, I'm afraid."

"My father made a new will on the occasion of his marriage two years ago," said Percival precisely. "My father left the sum of £100,000 to his wife absolutely and £50,000 to my sister, Elaine. I am his residuary legatee. I am already, of course, a partner in the firm."

"There was no bequest to your brother, Lancelot Fortescue?"

"No, there is an estrangement of long standing between my father and my brother."

Neele threw a sharp glance at him—but Percival seemed quite sure of his statement.

"So as the will stands," said Inspector Neele, "the three people who stand to gain are Mrs. Fortescue, Miss Elaine Fortescue and yourself?"

"I don't think I shall be much of a gainer." Percival sighed. "There are death duties, you know, Inspector.

And of late my father has been—well, all I can say is, highly injudicious in some of his financial dealings."

"You and your father have not seen eye to eye lately about the conduct of the business?" Inspector Neele threw out the question in a genial manner.

"I put my point of view to him, but alas—" Percival shrugged his shoulders.

"Put it rather forcibly, didn't you?" Neele inquired. "In fact, not to put too fine a point on it, there was quite a row about it, wasn't there?"

"I should hardly say that, Inspector." A red flush of annoyance mounted to Percival's forehead.

"Perhaps the dispute you had was about some other matter then, Mr. Fortescue."

"There was no dispute, Inspector."

"Quite sure of that, Mr. Fortescue? Well, no matter. Did I understand that your father and brother are still estranged?"

"That is so."

"Then perhaps you can tell me what this means?"

Neele handed him the telephone message Mary Dove had jotted down.

Percival read it and uttered an exclamation of surprise and annoyance. He seemed both incredulous and angry.

"I can't understand it, I really can't. I can hardly believe it."

"It seems to be true, though, Mr. Fortescue. Your brother is arriving from Paris today."

"But it's extraordinary, quite extraordinary. No, I really can't understand it."

"Your father said nothing to you about it?"

"He certainly did not. How outrageous of him. To go behind my back and send for Lance."

"You've no idea, I suppose, why he did such a thing?"

"Of course I haven't. It's all on a par with his behavior lately—crazy—unaccountable—it's got to be
stopped—I—"

Percival came to an abrupt stop. The color ebbed
away again from his pale face.

"I'd forgotten," he said. "For the moment I'd forgotten that my father was dead."

Inspector Neele shook his head sympathetically.

Percival Fortescue prepared to take his departure.
As he picked up his hat he said, "Call upon me if there
is anything I can do. But I suppose—" he paused—
"you will be coming down to Yewtree Lodge?"

"Yes, Mr. Fortescue. I've got a man in charge there
now."

Percival shuddered in a fastidious way.

"It will all be most unpleasant. To think such a
thing should happen to us—"

He sighed and moved towards the door.

"I shall be at the office most of the day. There is a lot
to be seen to here. But I shall get down to Yewtree
Lodge this evening."

"Quite so, sir."

Percival Fortescue went out.

"Percy Prim," murmured Neele.

Sergeant Hay, who was sitting unobtrusively by the
wall, looked up and said "Sir?" interrogatively.

Then, as Neele did not reply, he asked, "What do you
make of it all, sir?"

"I don't know," said Neele. He quoted softly,
" 'They're all very unpleasant people.' "

Sergeant Hay looked somewhat puzzled.

"Alice in Wonderland," said Neele. "Don't you know
your Alice, Hay?"

"It's a classic, isn't it, sir?" said Hay. "Third Program
stuff. I don't listen to the Third Program."

Chapter Ten

It was about five minutes after leaving Le Bourget that Lance Fortescue opened his copy of the continental *Daily Mail*. A minute or two later he uttered a startled exclamation. Pat, in the seat beside him, turned her head inquiringly.

"It's the old man," said Lance. "He's dead."

"Dead! Your father?"

"Yes, he seems to have been taken suddenly ill at the office, was taken to St. Jude's Hospital and died there soon after arrival."

"Darling, I'm so sorry. What was it, a stroke?"

"I suppose so. Sounds like it."

"Did he ever have a stroke before?"

"No. Not that I know of."

"I thought people never died from a first one."

"Poor old boy," said Lance. "I never thought I was particularly fond of him, but somehow, now that he's dead . . ."

"Of course you were fond of him."

"We haven't all got your nice nature, Pat. Oh well, it looks as though my luck's out again, doesn't it."

"Yes. It's odd that it should happen just now. Just when you were on the point of coming home."

He turned his head sharply towards her.

"Odd? What do you mean by odd, Pat?"

She looked at him with slight surprise.

"Well, a sort of coincidence."

"You mean that whatever I set out to do goes wrong?"

"No, darling, I didn't mean that. But there is such a thing as a run of bad luck."

"Yes, I suppose there is."

Pat said again, "I'm so sorry."

When they arrived at Heath Row and were waiting to disembark from the plane, an official of the air company called out in a clear voice:

"Is Mr. Lancelot Fortescue aboard?"

"Here," said Lance.

"Would you just step this way, Mr. Fortescue."

Lance and Pat followed him out of the plane, preceding the other passengers. As they passed a couple in the last seat, they heard the man whisper to his wife,

"Well-known smugglers, I expect. Caught in the act."

ii

"It's fantastic," said Lance. "Quite fantastic." He stared across the table at Detective Inspector Neele.

Inspector Neele nodded his head sympathetically.

"Taxine—yewberries—the whole thing seems like some kind of melodrama. I daresay this sort of thing seems ordinary enough to you, Inspector. All in the day's work. But poisoning, in our family, seems wildly farfetched."

"You've no idea then at all," asked Inspector Neele, "who might have poisoned your father?"

"Good Lord, no. I expect the old man's made a lot of enemies in business, lots of people who'd like to skin him alive, do him down financially—all that sort of thing. But poisoning? Anyway, I wouldn't be in the know. I've been abroad for a good many years and have known very little of what's going on at home."

"That's really what I wanted to ask you about, Mr. Fortescue. I understand from your brother that there was an estrangement between you and your father which had lasted for many years. Would you like to tell me the circumstances that led to your coming home at this time?"

"Certainly, Inspector. I heard from my father, let me see, it must be about—yes, six months ago now. It was soon after my marriage. My father wrote and hinted that he would like to let bygones be bygones. He suggested that I should come home and enter the firm. He was rather vague in his terms and I wasn't really sure that I wanted to do what he asked. Anyway, the upshot was that I came over to England last—yes, last August, just about three months ago. I went down to see him at Yewtree Lodge and he made me, I must say, a very advantageous offer. I told him that I'd have to think about it and I'd have to consult my wife. He quite understood that. I flew back to East Africa, talked it over with Pat. The upshot was that I decided to accept the old boy's offer. I had to wind up my affairs there, but I agreed to do so before the end of last month. I told him I would wire to him the date of my actual arrival in England."

Inspector Neele coughed.

"Your arrival back seems to have caused your brother some surprise."

Lance gave a sudden grin. His rather attractive face lit up with the spirit of pure mischief.

"Don't believe old Percy knew a thing about it," he said. "He was away on his holiday in Norway at the time. If you ask me, the old man picked that particular time on purpose. He was going behind Percy's back. In fact, I've a very shrewd suspicion that my father's offer to me was actuated by the fact that he had a blazing row with poor old Percy—or Val as he prefers to be called. Val, I think, had been more or less trying to run the old man. Well, the old man would never stand for anything of that kind. What the exact row was about I don't know, but he was furious. And I think he thought it a jolly good idea to get me there and thereby spike poor old Val. For one thing he never liked Percy's wife much and he was rather pleased, in a snobbish kind of way, with my marriage. It would be just his idea of a good joke to get me home and suddenly confront Percy with the accomplished fact."

"How long were you at Yewtree Lodge on this occasion?"

"Oh, not more than an hour or two. He didn't ask me to stay the night. The whole idea, I'm sure, was a kind of secret offensive behind Percy's back. I don't think he even wanted the servants to report upon it. As I say, things were left that I'd think it over, talk about it to Pat and then write him my decision, which I did. I wrote giving him the approximate date of my arrival, and I finally sent him a telegram yesterday from Paris."

Inspector Neele nodded.

"A telegram which surprised your brother very much."

"I bet it did. However, as usual, Percy wins. I've arrived too late."

"Yes," said Inspector Neele thoughtfully, "you've

arrived too late." He went on briskly, "On the occasion
of your visit last August, did you meet any other members of the family?"

"My stepmother was there at tea."

"You had not met her previously?"

"No." He grinned suddenly. "The old boy certainly
knew how to pick them. She must be thirty years
younger than he, at least."

"You will excuse my asking, but did you resent your
father's remarriage, or did your brother do so?"

Lance looked surprised.

"I certainly didn't, and I shouldn't think Percy did
either. After all, our own mother died when we were
about—oh, ten, twelve years old. What I'm really surprised at is that the old man didn't marry again before."

Inspector Neele murmured, "It may be considered
taking rather a risk to marry a woman very much
younger than yourself."

"Did my dear brother say that to you? It sounds
rather like him. Percy is a great master of the art of
insinuation. Is that the setup, Inspector? Is my stepmother suspected of poisoning my father?"

Inspector Neele's face became blank.

"It's early days to have any definite ideas about anything, Mr. Fortescue," he said pleasantly. "Now, may I
ask you what your plans are?"

"Plans?" Lance considered. "I shall have to make
new plans, I suppose. Where is the family? All down
at Yewtree Lodge?"

"Yes."

"I'd better go down there straightaway." He turned
to his wife. "You'd better go to a hotel, Pat."

She protested quickly. "No, no, Lance, I'll come with
you."

"No, darling."

"But I want to."

"Really, I'd rather you didn't. Go and stay at the—oh, it's so long since I stayed in London—Barnes'. Barnes' Hotel used to be a nice, quiet sort of place. That's still going, I suppose?"

"Oh, yes, Mr. Fortescue."

"Right, Pat, I'll settle you in there if they've got a room, then I'll go on down to Yewtree Lodge."

"But why can't I come with you, Lance?"

Lance's face took suddenly a rather grim line.

"Frankly, Pat, I'm not sure of my welcome. It was Father who invited me there, but Father's dead. I don't know whom the place belongs to now. Percy, I suppose, or perhaps Adele. Anyway, I'd like to see what reception I get before I bring you there. Besides—"

"Besides what?"

"I don't want to take you to a house where there's a poisoner at large."

"Oh, what nonsense."

Lance said firmly, "Where you're concerned, Pat, I'm taking no risks."

Chapter Eleven

Mr. Dubois was annoyed. He tore Adele Fortescue's letter angrily across and threw it into the wastepaper basket. Then, with a sudden caution, he fished out the various pieces, struck a match and watched them burn to ashes. He muttered under his breath, "Why have women got to be such damned fools? Surely common prudence . . ."

But then, Mr. Dubois reflected gloomily, women never had any prudence. Though he had profited by this lack many a time, it annoyed him now. He himself had taken every precaution. If Mrs. Fortescue rang up, they had instructions to say that he was out. Already Adele Fortescue had rung him up three times, and now she had written. On the whole, writing was far worse. He reflected for a moment or two, then went to the telephone.

"Can I speak to Mrs. Fortescue, please? Yes, Mr. Dubois." A minute or two later he heard her voice.

"Vivian, at last."

"Yes, yes, Adele, but be careful. Where are you speaking from?"

"From the library."

"Sure nobody's listening in, in the hall?"

"Why should they?"

"Well, you never know. Are the police still about the house?"

"No, they've gone for the moment, anyhow. Oh, Vivian dear, it's been awful."

"Yes, yes, it must have, I'm sure. But look here, Adele, we've got to be careful."

"Oh, of course, darling."

"Don't call me darling through the phone. It isn't safe."

"Aren't you being a little bit panicky, Vivian? After all, everybody says darling nowadays."

"Yes, yes, that's true enough. But listen. Don't telephone to me, and don't write."

"But, Vivian—"

"It's just for the present, you understand. We must be careful."

"Oh. All right." Her voice sounded offended.

"Adele, listen. My letters to you. You did burn them, didn't you?"

There was a momentary hesitation before Adele Fortescue said, "Of course. I told you I was going to do so."

"That's all right, then. Well, I'll ring off now. Don't phone and don't write. You'll hear from me in good time."

He put the receiver back on its hook. He stroked his cheek thoughtfully. He didn't like that moment's hesitation. Had Adele burnt his letters? Women were all the same. They promised to burn things and then didn't.

Letters, Mr. Dubois thought to himself. Women always wanted you to write them letters. He himself tried to be careful, but sometimes one could not get out of it. What had he said exactly in the few letters he had written to Adele Fortescue? It was the usual sort of gup, he thought, gloomily. But were there any special words—special phrases that the police could twist to make them say what they wanted them to say? He remembered the Edith Thompson case. His letters were innocent enough, he thought, but he could not be sure. His uneasiness grew. Even if Adele had not already burnt his letters, would she have the sense to burn them now? Or had the police already got hold of them? Where did she keep them, he wondered. Probably in the sitting-room of hers upstairs. That gimcrack little desk, probably. Sham antique Louis xiv. She had said something to him once about there being a secret drawer in it. Secret drawer! That would not fool the police long. But there were no police about the house now. She had said so. They had been there that morning, and now they had all gone away.

Up to now they had probably been busy looking for possible sources of poison in the food. They would not, he hoped, have got round to a room-by-room search of the house. Perhaps they would have to ask permission or get a search warrant to do that. It was possible that if he acted now, at once—

He visualized the house clearly in his mind's eye. It would be getting towards dusk. Tea would be brought in, either into the library or into the drawing-room. Everyone would be assembled downstairs and the servants would be having tea in the servants' hall. There would be no one upstairs on the first floor. Easy to walk up through the garden, skirting the yew hedges that provided such admirable cover. Then there was the little door at the side onto the terrace. That was never locked until just before bedtime. One could slip through there and, choosing one's moment, slip upstairs.

Vivian Dubois considered very carefully what it behooved him to do next. If Fortescue's death had been put down to a seizure or to a stroke, as surely it ought to have been, the position would be very different. As it was—Dubois murmured under his breath, "Better be safe than sorry."

ii.

Mary Dove came slowly down the big staircase. She paused a moment at the window on the half landing, from which she had seen Inspector Neele arrive on the preceding day. Now, as she looked out in the half-light, she noticed a man's figure just disappearing round the yew hedge. She wondered if it was Lancelot Fortescue, the prodigal son. He had, perhaps, dismissed his car at the gate and was wandering round the garden, recollecting old times there before tackling a possibly hostile family. Mary Dove felt rather sympathetic towards Lance. A half smile on her lips, she went on downstairs. In the hall she encountered Gladys, the maid, who jumped nervously at the sight of her.

"Was that the telephone I heard just now?" Mary asked. "Who was it?"

"Oh, that was a wrong number. Thought we were the laundry." Gladys sounded breathless and rather hurried. "And before that, it was Mr. Dubois. He wanted to speak to the mistress."

"I see."

Mary went on across the hall. Turning her head, she said, "It's teatime, I think. Haven't you brought it in yet?"

Gladys said, "I don't think it's half-past four yet, is it, miss?"

"It's twenty minutes to five. Bring it in now, will you?"

Mary Dove went on into the library where Adele Fortescue, sitting on the sofa, was staring at the fire, picking with her fingers at a small lace handkerchief. Adele said fretfully, "Where's tea?"

Mary Dove said, "It's just coming in."

A log had fallen out of the fireplace, and Mary Dove knelt down at the grate and replaced it with the tongs, adding another piece of wood and a little coal.

Gladys went out into the kitchen where Mrs. Crump raised a red and wrathful face from the kitchen table where she was mixing pastry in a large bowl.

"The library bell's been ringing and ringing. Time you took in the tea, my girl."

"All right, all right, Mrs. Crump."

"What I'll say to Crump tonight," muttered Mrs. Crump. "I'll tell him off."

Gladys went on into the pantry. She had not cut any sandwiches. Well, she jolly well wasn't going to cut sandwiches. They'd got plenty to eat without that, hadn't they? Two cakes, biscuits, and scones and honey. Fresh, black-market farm butter. Plenty without her bothering to cut tomato or *foie gras* sandwiches. She'd got other things to think about. Fair temper Mrs. Crump was in, all because Mr. Crump had gone out this afternoon. Well, it was his day out, wasn't it? Quite right of him, Gladys thought.

Mrs. Crump called out from the kitchen, "The kettle's boiling its head off. Aren't you ever going to make that tea?"

"Coming."

She jerked some tea without measuring it into the big silver pot, carried the pot into the kitchen and poured the boiling water into it. She added the teapot and the kettle to the big silver tray and carried the whole thing through to the library where she set it on the small table near the sofa. She went back hurriedly for the other tray with the eatables on it. She carried the latter as far as the hall when the sudden jarring noise of the grand-father clock preparing itself to strike made her jump.

In the library, Adele Fortescue said querulously to Mary Dove, "Where is everybody this afternoon?"

"I really don't know, Mrs. Fortescue. Miss Fortescue came in some time ago. I think Mrs. Percival's writing letters in her room."

Adele said pettishly, "Writing letters, writing letters. That woman never stops writing letters. She's like all people of her class. She takes an absolute delight in death and misfortune. Ghoulish, that's what I call it. Absolutely ghoulish."

Mary murmured tactfully, "I'll tell her that tea is ready."

Going towards the door, she drew back a little in the doorway as Elaine Fortescue came into the room.

Elaine said, "It's cold," and dropped down by the fireplace, rubbing her hands before the blaze.

Mary stood for a moment in the hall. A large tray with cakes on it was standing on one of the hall chests. Since it was getting dark in the hall, Mary switched on the light. As she did so, she thought she heard Jennifer Fortescue walking along the passage upstairs. Nobody, however, came down the stairs, and Mary went up the staircase and along the corridor.

Percival Fortescue and his wife occupied a self-contained suite in one wing of the house. Mary tapped on the sitting-room door. Mrs. Percival liked you to tap on doors, a fact which always roused Crump's scorn of her. Her voice said briskly, "Come in."

Mary opened the door and murmured, "Tea is just coming in, Mrs. Percival."

She was rather surprised to see Jennifer Fortescue with her outdoor clothes on. She was just divesting herself of a long, camel-hair coat.

"I didn't know you'd been out," said Mary.

Mrs. Percival sounded slightly out of breath.

"Oh, I was just in the garden, that's all. Just getting a little air. Really, though, it was too cold. I shall be glad to get down to the fire. The central heating here isn't as good as it might be. Somebody must speak to the gardeners about it, Miss Dove."

"I'll do so," Mary promised.

Jennifer Fortescue dropped her coat on a chair and followed Mary out of the room. She went down the stairs ahead of Mary, who drew back a little to give her precedence. In the hall, rather to Mary's surprise, she noticed the tray of eatables was still there. She was about to go out to the pantry and call to Gladys when Adele Fortescue appeared in the door to the library, saying in an irritable voice, "Aren't we ever going to have anything to eat for tea?"

Quickly Mary picked up the tray and took it into the library, disposing the various things on low tables near the fireplace. She was carrying the empty tray out to the hall again when the front doorbell rang. Setting down the tray, Mary went to the door herself. If this was the prodigal son at last, she was rather curious to see him. How unlike the rest of the Fortescues, Mary thought, as she opened the door and looked up into the dark, lean face and the faintly quizzical twist of the mouth. She said quietly, "Mr. Lancelot Fortescue?"

"Himself."

Mary peered beyond him.

"Your luggage?"

"I've paid off the taxi. This is all I've got."

He picked up a medium-sized zip bag. Some faint feeling of surprise in her mind, Mary said, "Oh, you did come in a taxi. I thought perhaps you'd walked up. And your wife?"

His face set in a rather grim line, Lance said, "My wife won't be coming. At least, not just yet."

"I see. Come this way, will you, Mr. Fortescue? Everyone is in the library, having tea,"

She took him to the library door and left him there. She thought to herself that Lancelot Fortescue was a very attractive person. A second thought followed the first. Probably a great many other women thought so, too.

iii

"Lance!"

Elaine came hurrying forward towards him. She flung her arms round his neck and hugged him with a schoolgirl abandon that Lance found quite surprising.

"Hullo. Here I am."

He disengaged himself gently.

"This is Jennifer?"

Jennifer Fortescue looked at him with eager curiosity.

"I'm afraid Val's been detained in town," she said. "There's so much to see to, you know. All the arrangements to make and everything. Of course it all comes on Val. He has to see to everything. You can really have no idea what we're all going through."

"It must be terrible for you," said Lance gravely.

He turned to the woman on the sofa, who was sitting with a piece of scone and honey in her hand, quietly appraising him.

"Of course," cried Jennifer, "you don't know Adele, do you?"

Lance murmured "Oh yes, I do" as he took Adele Fortescue's hand in his. As he looked down at her, her eyelids fluttered. She set down the scone she was eating with her left hand and just touched the arrangement of her hair. It was a feminine gesture. It marked her recognition of the entry to the room of a personable man. She said in her thick, soft voice, "Sit down here on the sofa beside me, Lance." She poured out a cup of tea for him. "I'm so glad you've come," she went on. "We badly need another man in the house."

Lance said, "You must let me do everything I can to help."

"You know—but perhaps you don't know—we've had the police here. They think—they think—" she broke off and cried out passionately, "Oh, it's awful! Awful!"

"I know." Lance was grave and sympathetic. "As a matter of fact, they met me at London Airport."

"The police met you?"

"Yes."

"What did they say?"

"Well," Lance was deprecating, "they told me what had happened."

"He was poisoned," said Adele, "that's what they think, what they say. Not food poisoning. Real poisoning, by someone. I believe, I really do believe they think it's one of us."

Lance gave her a sudden, quick smile.

"That's their pigeon," he said consolingly. "It's no good our worrying. What a scrumptious tea! It's a long time since I've seen a good English tea."

The others fell in with his mood soon enough. Adele said suddenly, "But your wife—haven't you got a wife, Lance?"

"I've got a wife, yes. She's in London."

"But aren't you—hadn't you better bring her down here?"

"Plenty of time to make plans," said Lance. "Pat—oh, Pat's quite all right where she is."

Elaine said sharply,

"You don't mean—you don't think—"

Lance said quickly, "What a wonderful-looking chocolate cake. I must have some." Cutting himself a slice, he asked, "Is Aunt Effie alive still?"

"Oh, yes, Lance. She won't come down and have meals with us or anything, but she's quite well. Only, she's getting very peculiar."

"She always was peculiar," said Lance. "I must go up and see her after tea."

Jennifer Fortescue murmured, "At her age one does really feel that she ought to be in some kind of a home. I mean somewhere where she will be properly looked after."

"Heaven help any old ladies' home that got Aunt Effie in their midst," said Lance. He added, "Who's the demure piece of goods who let me in?"

Adele looked surprised.

"Didn't Crump let you in? The butler? Oh no, I forgot. It's his day out today. But surely Gladys—"

Lance gave a description. "Blue eyes, hair parted in the middle, soft voice, butter wouldn't melt in the mouth. What goes on behind it all, I wouldn't like to say."

"That," said Jennifer, "would be Mary Dove."

Elaine said, "She sort of runs things for us."

"Does she, now."

Adele said, "She's really very useful."

"Yes," said Lance thoughtfully, "I should think she might be."

"But what is so nice is," said Jennifer, "that she

knows her place. She never presumes, if you know what I mean."

"Clever Mary Dove," said Lance, and helped himself to another piece of chocolate cake.

Chapter Twelve

"So you've turned up again like a bad penny," said Miss Ramsbottom.

Lance grinned at her. "Just as you say, Aunt Effie."

"Humph!" Miss Ramsbottom sniffed disapprovingly. "You've chosen a nice time to do it. Your father got himself murdered yesterday, the house is full of police poking about everywhere, grubbing in the dustbins, even. I've seen them out of the window." She paused, sniffed again, and asked, "Got your wife with you?"

"No. I left Pat in London."

"That shows some sense. I shouldn't bring her here if I were you. You never know what might happen."

"To her? To Pat?"

"To anybody," said Miss Ramsbottom.

Lance Fortescue looked at her thoughtfully.

"Got any ideas about it all, Aunt Effie?" he asked.

Miss Rambottom did not reply directly. "I had an Inspector here yesterday asking me questions. He didn't get much change out of me. But he wasn't such a fool as he looked, not by a long way." She added with some indignation, "What your grandfather would feel if he knew we had the police in the house—it's enough to make him turn in his grave. A strict Plymouth Brother he was all his life. The fuss there was when he found out I'd been attending Church of England services in the evening! And I'm sure that was harmless enough compared to murder."

Normally Lance would have smiled at this, but his long, dark face remained serious. He said, "D'you know, I'm quite in the dark after having been away so long. What's been going on here of late?"

Miss Ramsbottom raised her eyes to heaven.

"Godless doings," she said firmly.

"Yes, yes, Aunt Effie, you would say that anyway. But what gives the police the idea that Dad was killed here, in this house?"

"Adultery is one thing and murder is another," said Miss Ramsbottom. "I shouldn't like to think it of her, I shouldn't, indeed."

Lance looked alert. "Adele?" he asked.

"My lips are sealed," said Miss Ramsbottom.

"Come on, old dear," said Lance. "It's a lovely phrase, but it doesn't mean a thing. Adele had a boy friend? Adele and the boy friend fed him henbane in the morning tea. Is that the setup?"

"I'll trouble you not to joke about it."

"I wasn't really joking, you know."

"I'll tell you one thing," said Miss Ramsbottom suddenly. "I believe that girl knows something about it."

"Which girl?" Lance looked surprised.

"The one that sniffs," said Miss Ramsbottom. "The one that ought to have brought me up my tea this afternoon, but didn't. Gone out without leave, so they say. Well, shouldn't wonder if she had gone to the police. Who let you in?"

"Someone called Mary Dove, I understand. Very meek and mild, but not really. Is she the one who's gone to the police?"

"She wouldn't go to the police," said Miss Ramsbottom. "No—I mean that silly little parlormaid. She's been twitching and jumping like a rabbit all day. 'What's the matter with you?' I said. 'Have you got a guilty conscience?' She said, 'I never did anything—I wouldn't do a thing like that.' 'I hope you wouldn't,' I said to her, 'but there's something worrying you now, isn't there?' Then she began to sniff and said she didn't want to get anybody into trouble, she was sure it must be all a mistake. I said to her, I said, 'Now, my girl, you speak the truth and shame the devil.' That's what I said. 'You go to the police,' I said, 'and tell them anything you know, because no good ever came,' I said, 'of hushing up the truth, however unpleasant it is.' Then she talked a lot of nonsense about how she couldn't go to the police, they'd never believe her and what on earth should she say? She ended up by saying anyway she didn't know anything at all."

"You don't think," Lance hesitated, "that she was just making herself important?"

"No, I don't. I think she was scared. I think she saw something or heard something that's given her some idea about the whole thing. It may be important, or it mayn't be of the least consequence."

"You don't think she herself could've had a grudge against Father and—" Lance hesitated.

Miss Ramsbottom was shaking her head decidedly.

"She's not the kind of girl your father would have taken the least notice of. No man ever will take much notice of her, poor girl. Ah, well, it's all the better for her soul, that, I dare say."

Lance took no interest in Gladys's soul. He asked,

"You think she may have run along to the police station?"

Aunt Effie nodded vigorously.

"Yes. I think she mayn't like to've said anything to them in this house, in case somebody overheard her."

Lance asked, "Do you think she may have seen someone tampering with the food?"

Aunt Effie threw him a sharp glance.

"It's possible, isn't it?" she said.

"Yes, I suppose so." Then he added apologetically, "The whole thing still seems so wildly improbable. Like a detective story."

"Percival's wife is a hospital nurse," said Miss Ramsbottom.

The remark seemed so unconnected with what had gone before that Lance looked at her in a puzzled fashion.

"Hospital nurses are used to handling drugs," said Miss Ramsbottom.

Lance looked doubtful.

"This stuff—taxine—is it ever used in medicine?"

"They get it from yewberries, I gather. Children eat yewberries sometimes," said Miss Ramsbottom. "Makes them very ill, too. I remember a case when I was a child. It made a great impression on me. I never forgot it. Things you remember come in useful sometimes."

Lance raised his head sharply and stared at her.

"Natural affection is one thing," said Miss Ramsbottom, "and I hope I've got as much of it as anyone. But I won't stand for wickedness. Wickedness has to be destroyed."

ii.

"Went off without a word to me," said Mrs. Crump, raising her red, wrathful face from the pastry she was now rolling out on the board. "Slipped out without a word to anybody. Sly, that's what it is. Sly! Afraid she'd be stopped, and I would have stopped her if I'd caught her! The idea! There's the master dead, Mr. Lance coming home that hasn't been home for years, and I said to Crump, I said, 'Day out or no day out, I know my duty. There's not going to be cold supper tonight as is usual on a Thursday, but a proper dinner. A gentleman coming home from abroad with his wife, what was formerly married in the aristocracy, things must be properly done.' You know me, miss, you know I take a pride in my work."

Mary Dove, the recipient of these confidences, nodded her head gently.

"And what does Crump say?" Mrs. Crump's voice rose angrily. " 'It's my day off and I'm goin' off,' that's what he says. 'And a fig for the aristocracy,' he says. No pride in his work, Crump hasn't. So off he goes and I tell Gladys she'll have to manage alone tonight. She just says, 'All right, Mrs. Crump,' then, when my back's turned out she sneaks. It wasn't her day out, anyway. Friday's her day. How we're going to manage now, I don't know. Thank goodness, Mr. Lance hasn't brought his wife here with him today."

"We shall manage, Mrs. Crump," Mary's voice was both soothing and authoritative, "if we just simplify the menu a little." She outlined a few suggestions. Mrs. Crump nodded unwilling acquiescence. "I shall be able to serve that quite easily," Mary concluded.

"You mean you'll wait at table yourself, miss?" Mrs. Crump sounded doubtful.

"If Gladys doesn't come back in time."

"She won't come back," said Mrs. Crump. "Gallivanting off, wasting her money somewhere in the shops. She's got a young man, you know, miss, though you wouldn't think it to look at her. Albert his name is.

Going to get married next spring, so she tells me. Don't know what the married state's like, these girls don't. What I've been through with Crump." She sighed, then said in an ordinary voice, "What about tea, miss? Who's going to clear it away and wash it up?"

"I'll do that," said Mary. "I'll go and do it now."

The lights had not been turned on in the drawing-room, though Adele Fortescue was still sitting on the sofa behind the tea tray.

"Shall I switch the lights on, Mrs. Fortescue?" Mary asked. Adele did not answer.

Mary switched on the lights and went across to the window where she pulled the curtains across. It was only then that she turned her head and saw the face of the woman who had sagged back against the cushions. A half-eaten scone spread with honey was beside her and her tea cup was still half-full. Death had come to Adele Fortescue suddenly and swiftly.

iii.

"Well?" demanded Inspector Neele impatiently.

The doctor said promptly,

"Cyanide—potassium cyanide probably—in the tea."

"Cyanide," muttered Neele.

The doctor looked at him with slight curiosity.

"You're taking this hard. Any special reason?"

"She was cast as a murderess," said Neele.

"And she turns out to be a victim. Hm. You'll have to think again, won't you?"

Neele nodded. His face was bitter and his jaw was grimly set.

Poisoned! Right under his nose. Taxine in Rex Fortescue's breakfast coffee, cyanide in Adele Fortescue's tea. Still an intimate family affair. Or so it seemed.

Adele Fortescue, Jennifer Fortescue, Elaine Fortescue and the newly arrived Lance Fortescue had had tea together in the library. Lance had gone up to see Miss Ramsbottom, Jennifer had gone to her own sitting-room to write letters, Elaine had been the last to leave the library. According to her, Adele had then been in perfect health and had just been pouring herself out a last cup of tea.

A last cup of tea! Yes, it had indeed been her last cup of tea.

And after that a blank twenty minutes, perhaps, until Mary Dove had come into the room and discovered the body.

And during that twenty minutes—

Inspector Neele swore to himself and went out into the kitchen.

Sitting in a chair by the kitchen table, the vast figure of Mrs. Crump, her belligerence pricked like a balloon, hardly stirred as he came in.

"Where's that girl? Has she come back yet?"

"Gladys? No, she's not back. Won't be, I suspect, until eleven o'clock."

"She made the tea, you say, and took it in."

"I didn't touch it, sir, as God's my witness. And what's more, I don't believe Gladys did anything she shouldn't. She wouldn't do a thing like that—not Gladys. She's a good enough girl, sir—a bit foolish like, that's all—not wicked."

No, Neele did not think that Gladys was wicked. He did not think that Gladys was a poisoner. And in any case the cynanide had not been in the teapot.

"But what made her go off suddenly—like this? It wasn't her day out, you say."

"No, sir, tomorrow's her day out."

"Does Crump—"

Mrs. Crump's belligerence suddenly revived. Her voice rose wrathfully.

"Don't you go fastening anything on Crump. Crump's out of it. He went off at three o'clock—and thankful I am now that he did. He's as much out of it as Mr. Percival himself."

Percival Fortescue had only just returned from London—to be greeted by the astounding news of this second tragedy.

"I wasn't accusing Crump," said Neele mildly. "I just wondered if he knew anything about Gladys's plans."

"She had her best nylons on," said Mrs. Crump. "She was up to something. Don't tell me! Didn't cut any sandwiches for tea, either. Oh yes, she was up to something. I'll give her a piece of my mind when she comes back."

When she comes back—

A faint uneasiness possessed Neele. To shake it off, he went upstairs to Adele Fortescue's bedroom. A lavish apartment—all rose brocade hangings and a vast gilt bed. On one side of the room was a door into a mirror-lined bathroom with a sunken, orchid pink porcelain bath. Beyond the bathroom, reached by a communicating door, was Rex Fortescue's room. Neele went back into Adele's bedroom, and through the door on the farther side of the room into her sitting-room.

The room was furnished in Empire style with a rose pile carpet. Neele only gave it a cursory glance, for that particular room had had his close attention on the preceding day—with special attention paid to the small, elegant desk.

Now, however, he stiffened to sudden attention. On the center of the rose pile carpet was a small piece of caked mud.

Neele went over to it and picked it up. The mud was still damp.

He looked round—there were no footprints visible—only this one, isolated fragment of wet earth.

iv.

Inspector Neele looked round the bedroom that belonged to Gladys Martin. It was past eleven o'clock. Crump had come in half an hour ago, but there was still no sign of Gladys. Inspector Neele looked round him. Whatever Gladys's training had been, her own natural instincts were slovenly. The bed, Inspector Neele judged, was seldom made, the windows seldom opened. Gladys's personal habits, however, were not his immediate concern. Instead, he went carefully through her possessions.

They consisted, for the most part, of cheap and rather pathetic finery. There was little that was durable or of good quality. The elderly Ellen, whom he had called upon to assist him, had not been helpful. She didn't know what clothes Gladys had or hadn't. She couldn't say what, if anything, was missing. He turned from the clothes and the underclothes to the contents of the chest of drawers. There Gladys kept her treasures. There were picture post cards and newspaper cuttings, knitting patterns, hints on beauty culture, dressmaking and fashion advice.

Inspector Neele sorted them neatly into various categories. The picture post cards consisted mainly of views of various places where he presumed Gladys had spent her holidays. Among them were three picture post cards signed "Bert." Bert he took to be the "young man" referred to by Mrs. Crump. The first post card said, in an illiterate hand, "All the best. Missing you a lot. Yours ever, Bert." The second said, "Lots of nice-looking girls here but not one that's a patch on you. Be seeing you soon. Don't forget our date. And remember after that—it's thumbs up and living happy ever after."

The third said merely. "Don't forget. I'm trusting you. Love, B."

Next, Neele looked through the newspaper cuttings and sorted them into three piles. There were the dressmaking and beauty hints, there were items about cinema stars to which Gladys had appeared greatly addicted, and she had also, it appeared, been attracted by the latest marvels of science. There were cuttings about flying saucers, about secret weapons, about truth drugs used by Russians, and claims for fantastic drugs discovered by American doctors. All the witchcraft, so Neele thought, of our twentieth century. But in all the contents of the room there was nothing to give him a clue to her disappearance. She had kept no diary, not that he had expected that. It was a remote possibility. There was no unfinished letter, no record at all of anything she might have seen in the house which could have had a bearing on Rex Fortescue's death. Whatever Gladys had seen, whatever Gladys had known, there was no record of it. It would still have to be guesswork why the second tea tray had been left in the hall, and Gladys herself had so suddenly vanished.

Sighing, Neele left the room, shutting the door behind him.

As he prepared to descend the small, winding stairs he heard a noise of running feet coming along the landing below.

The agitated face of Sergeant Hay looked up at him from the bottom of the stairs. Sergeant Hay was panting a little.

"Sir," he said urgently, "Sir! We've found her."

"Found her?"

"It was the housemaid, sir—Ellen—remembered as she hadn't brought the clothes in from where they were hanging on the line—just round the corner from the back door. So she went out with a torch to take them

in and she almost fell over the body—the girl's body—
strangled, she was, with a stocking round her throat—
been dead for hours, I'd say. And, sir, it's a wicked
kind of joke—there was a clothes peg clipped on her
nose—"

Chapter Thirteen

An elderly lady traveling by train had bought three morning papers, and each of them, as she finished it, folded it and laid it aside, showed the same headline. It was no longer a question now of a small paragraph hidden away in the corner of the papers. There were headlines with flaring announcements of Triple Tragedy at Yewtree Lodge.

The old lady sat very upright, looking out of the window of the train, her lips pursed together, an expression of distress and disapproval on her pink and white wrinkled face. Miss Marple had left St. Mary Meade by the early train, changing at the junction and going on to London where she took a Circle train to another London terminus and thence on to Baydon Heath.

At the station she signaled a taxi and asked to be taken to Yewtree Lodge. So charming, so innocent, such a fluffy and pink and white old lady was Miss Marple that she gained admittance to what was now practically a fortress in a state of siege far more easily than could have been believed possible. Though an army of reporters and photographers was being kept at bay by the police, Miss Marple was allowed to drive in without question, so impossible would it have been to believe that she was anyone but an elderly relative of the family.

Miss Marple paid off the taxi in a careful assortment of small change, and rang the front doorbell. Crump opened it and Miss Marple summed him up with an experienced glance. A shifty eye, she said to herself. Scared to death, too.

Crump saw a tall, elderly lady wearing an old-fashioned tweed coat and skirt, a couple of scarves and a small felt hat with a bird's wing. The old lady carried a capacious handbag, and an aged but good quality suitcase reposed by her feet.

Crump recognized a lady when he saw one and said, "Yes, madam?" in his best and most respectful voice.

"Could I see the mistress of the house, please?" said Miss Marple.

Crump drew back to let her in. He picked up the suitcase and put it carefully down in the hall.

"Well, madam," he said rather dubiously, "I don't know who exactly—"

Miss Marple helped him out.

"I have come," she said, "to speak about the poor girl who was killed. Gladys Martin."

"Oh, I see, madam. Well, in that case—" he broke off, and looked towards the library door from which a tall young woman had just emerged. "This is Mrs. Lance Fortescue, madam," he said.

Pat came forward, and she and Miss Marple looked at each other. Miss Marple was aware of a faint feeling of surprise. She had not expected to see someone like Patricia Fortescue in this particular house. Its interior was much as she had pictured it, but Pat did not some-how match with that interior.

"It's about Gladys, madam," said Crump helpfully.

Pat said rather hesitatingly, "Will you come in here? We shall be quite alone."

She led the way into the library and Miss Marple followed her.

"There wasn't anyone specially you wanted to see, was there?" said Pat. "Because perhaps I shan't be much good. You see, my husband and I only came back from Africa a few days ago. We don't really know anything about the household. But I can fetch my sister-in-law or my brother-in-law's wife."

Miss Marple looked at the girl and liked her. She liked her gravity and her simplicity. For some strange reason she felt sorry for her. A background of shabby chintz and horses and dogs, Miss Marple felt vaguely, would have been much more suitable than this richly furnished interior décor. At the pony show and gym-khanas held locally round St. Mary Meade, Miss Marple had met many Pats and knew them well. She felt at home with this rather unhappy-looking girl.

"It's very simple, really," said Miss Marple, taking off her gloves carefully and smoothing out the fingers of them. "I read in the paper, you see, about Gladys Martin having been killed. And of course I know all about her. She comes from my part of the country. I trained her, in fact, for domestic service. And since this terrible thing has happened to her, I felt—well, I felt that I ought to come and see if there was anything I could do about it."

"Yes," said Pat. "Of course. I see."

And she did see. Miss Marple's action appeared to her natural and inevitable.

"I think it's a very good thing you have come," said

Pat. "Nobody seems to know very much about her. I mean relations and all that."

"No," said Miss Marple, "of course not. She hadn't got any relations. She came to me from the orphanage. St. Faith's. A very well-run place, though sadly short of funds. We do our best for the girls there, try to give them a good training and all that. Gladys came to me when she was seventeen, and I taught her how to wait at table and keep the silver and everything like that. Of course, she didn't stay long. They never do. As soon as she got a little experience, she went and took a job in a café. The girls nearly always want to do that. They think it's freer, you know, and a gayer life. Perhaps it may be. I really don't know."

"I never even saw her," said Pat. "Was she a pretty girl?"

"Oh, no," said Miss Marple, "not at all. Adenoids, and a good many spots. She was rather pathetically stupid, too. I don't suppose," went on Miss Marple thoughtfully, "that she ever made many friends anywhere. She was very keen on men, poor girl. But men didn't take much notice of her, and other girls rather made use of her."

"It sounds rather cruel," said Pat.

"Yes, my dear," said Miss Marple, "life is cruel, I'm afraid. One doesn't really know what to do with the Gladyses. They enjoy going to the pictures and all that, but they're always thinking of impossible things that can't possibly happen to them. Perhaps that's happiness of a kind. But they get disappointed. I think Gladys was disappointed in café and restaurant life. Nothing very glamorous or interesting happened to her and it was just hard on the feet. Probably that's why she came back into private service. Do you know how long she'd been here?"

Pat shook her head.

"Not very long, I should think. Only a month or two." Pat paused and then went on, "It seems so horrible and futile that she should have been caught up in this thing. I suppose she'd seen something or noticed something."

"It was the clothes peg that really worried me," said Miss Marple in her gentle voice.

"The clothes peg?"

"Yes. I read about it in the papers. I suppose it is true? That when she was found there was a clothes peg clipped onto her nose."

Pat nodded. The color rose to Miss Marple's pink cheeks.

"That's what made me so very angry, if you can understand, my dear. It was such a cruel, contemptuous gesture. It gave me a kind of picture of the murderer. To do a thing like that! It's very wicked, you know, to affront human dignity. Particularly if you've already killed."

Pat said slowly,

"I think I see what you mean." She got up. "I think you'd better come and see Inspector Neele. He's in charge of the case, and he's here now. You'll like him, I think. He's a very human person." She gave a sudden, quick shiver. "The whole thing is such a horrible nightmare. Pointless. Mad. Without rhyme or reason in it."

"I wouldn't say that, you know," said Miss Marple. "No, I wouldn't say that."

Inspector Neele was looking tired and haggard. Three deaths, and the press of the whole country whooping down the trail. A case that seemed to be shaping in well-known fashion had gone suddenly haywire. Adele Fortescue, the appropriate suspect, was now the second victim of an incomprehensible murder case. At the close of that fatal day the Assistant Commissioner had sent for Neele, and the two men had talked far into the night.

In spite of his dismay, or rather behind it, Inspector Neele had felt a faint inward satisfaction. That pattern of the wife and the lover. It had been too slick, too easy. He had always mistrusted it. And now that mistrust of his was justified.

"The whole thing takes on an entirely different aspect," the A.C. had said, striding up and down his room and frowning. "It looks to me, Neele, as though we'd got someone mentally unhinged to deal with. First the husband, then the wife. But the very circumstances of the case seem to show that it's an inside job. It's all there, in the family. Someone who sat down to breakfast with Fortescue put taxine in his coffee or on his food. Someone who had tea with the family that day put potassium cyanide in Adele Fortescue's cup of tea. Someone trusted, unnoticed, one of the family. Which of 'em, Neele?"

Neele said dryly,

"Percival wasn't there, so that lets him out again. That lets him out again," Inspector Neele repeated.

The A.C. looked at him sharply. Something in the repetition had attracted his attention.

"What's the idea, Neele? Out with it, man."

Inspector Neele looked stolid.

"Nothing sir. Not so much as an idea. All I say is it was very convenient for him."

"A bit too convenient, eh?" The A.C. reflected and shook his head. "You think he might have managed it somehow? Can't see how, Neele. No, I can't see how."

He added, "And he's a cautious type, too."

"But quite intelligent, sir."

"You don't fancy the women. Is that it? Yet the women are indicated. Elaine Fortescue and Percival's wife. They were at breakfast and they were at tea that day. Either of them could have done it. No signs of anything abnormal about them? Well, it doesn't always show. There might be something in their past medical record."

Inspector Neele did not answer. He was thinking of Mary Dove. He had no definite reason for suspecting her, but that was the way his thoughts lay. There was something unexplained about her, unsatisfactory. A faint, amused antagonism. That had been her attitude after the death of Rex Fortescue. What was her attitude now? Her behavior and manner were, as always, exemplary. There was no longer, he thought, amusement. Perhaps not even antagonism, but he wondered whether, once or twice, he had not seen a trace of fear. He had been to blame, culpably to blame, in the matter of Gladys Martin. That slight, guilty confusion of hers he had put down to no more than a natural nervousness of the police. He had come across that guilty nervousness so often. In this case it had been something more. Gladys had seen or heard something which had aroused her suspicions. It was probably, he thought, some quite small thing, something so vague and indefinite that she had hardly liked to speak about it. And now, poor little rabbit, she would never speak.

Inspector Neele looked with some interest at the mild, earnest face of the old lady who confronted him now at Yewtree Lodge. He had been in two minds at first how to treat her, but he quickly made up his mind. Miss Marple would be useful to him. She was upright, of unimpeachable rectitude and she had, like most old ladies, time on her hands and an old maid's nose for scenting bits of gossip. She'd get things out of servants and out of the women of the Fortescue family, perhaps, that he and his policemen would never get. Talk, conjecture, reminiscences, repetitions of things said and done, out of them all she would pick the salient facts. So Inspector Neele was gracious.

"It's uncommonly good of you to have come here, Miss Marple," he said.

"It was my duty, Inspector Neele. The girl had lived in my house. I feel, in a sense, responsible for her. She was a very silly girl, you know."

Inspector Neele looked at her appreciatively.

"Yes," he said, "just so."

She had gone, he felt, to the heart of the matter.

"She wouldn't know," said Miss Marple, "what she ought to do. If, I mean, something came up. Oh, dear, I'm expressing myself very badly."

Inspector Neele said that he understood.

"She hadn't got good judgment as to what was important or not, that's what you mean, isn't it?"

"Oh yes, exactly, Inspector."

"When you say she was silly——" Inspector Neele broke off.

Miss Marple took up the theme.

"She was the credulous type. She was the sort of girl who would have given her savings to a swindler, if she'd had any savings. Of course, she never did have any savings because she always spent her money on most unsuitable clothes."

"What about men?" asked the Inspector.

"She wanted a young man badly," said Miss Marple. "In fact, that's really, I think, why she left St. Mary Meade. The competition there is very keen. So few men. She did have hopes of the young man who delivered the fish. Young Fred had a pleasant word for all the girls, but of course he didn't mean anything by it. That upset poor Gladys quite a lot. Still, I gather she did get herself a young man in the end?"

Inspector Neele nodded.

"It seems so. Albert Evans, I gather, his name was.

She seems to have met him at some holiday camp. He didn't give her a ring or anything, so maybe she made it all up. He was a mining engineer, so she told the cook."

"That seems most unlikely," said Miss Marple, "but I dare say it's what he told her. As I say, she'd believe anything. You don't connect him with this business at all?"

Inspector Neele shook his head.

"No. I don't think there are any complications of that kind. He never seems to have visited her. He sent her a post card from time to time, usually from a seaport. Probably Fourth Engineer on a boat on the Baltic run."

"Well," said Miss Marple, "I'm glad she had her little romance. Since her life has been cut short in this way—" She tightened her lips. "You know, Inspector, it makes me very, very angry." And she added, as she had said to Pat Fortescue, "Especially the clothes peg. That, Inspector, was really wicked."

Inspector Neele looked at her with interest.

"I know just what you mean, Miss Marple," he said.

Miss Marple coughed apologetically.

"I wonder—I suppose it would be great presumption on my part—if only I could assist you in my very humble and, I'm afraid, very feminine way. This is a wicked murderer, Inspector Neele, and the wicked should not go unpunished."

"That's an unfashionable belief nowadays, Miss Marple," Inspector Neele said rather grimly. "Not that I don't agree with you."

"There is a hotel near the station, or there's the Golf Hotel," said Miss Marple tentatively, "and I believe there's a Miss Ramsbottom in this house who is interested in foreign missions."

Inspector Neele looked at Miss Marple appraisingly.

"Yes," he said. "You've got something there, maybe. I can't say that I've had great success with the lady."

"It's really very kind of you, Inspector Neele," said Miss Marple. "I'm so glad you don't think I'm just a sensation hunter."

Inspector Neele gave a sudden, rather unexpected smile. He was thinking to himself that Miss Marple was very unlike the popular idea of an avenging fury. And yet, he thought, that was perhaps exactly what she was.

"Newspapers," said Miss Marple, "are often so sensational in their accounts. But hardly, I fear, as accurate as one might wish." She looked inquiringly at Inspector Neele. "If one could be sure of having just the sober facts."

"They're not particularly sober," said Neele. "Shorn of undue sensation, they're as follows. Mr. Fortescue died in his office as a result of taxine poisoning. Taxine is obtained from the berries and leaves of yew trees."

"Very convenient," Miss Marple said.

"Possibly," said Inspector Neele, "but we've no evidence as to that. As yet, that is." He stressed the point because it was here that he thought Miss Marple might be useful. If any brew or concoction of yewberries had been made in the house, Miss Marple was quite likely to come upon traces of it. She was the sort of old pussy who would make homemade liquors, cordials and herb teas herself. She would know methods of making and methods of disposal.

"And Mrs. Fortescue?"

"Mrs. Fortescue had tea with the family in the library. The last person to leave the room and the tea table was Miss Elaine Fortescue, her step-daughter. She states that as she left the room Mrs. Fortescue was pouring herself out another cup of tea. Some twenty minutes or half-hour later Miss Dove, who acts as housekeeper, went in to remove the tea tray. Mrs. Fortescue was still sitting on the sofa, dead. Beside her was a tea cup a quarter full, and in the dregs of it was potassium cyanide."

"Which is almost immediate in its action, I believe," said Miss Marple.

"Exactly."

"Such dangerous stuff," murmured Miss Marple. "One has it to take wasps' nests but I'm always very, very careful."

"You're quite right," said Inspector Neele. "There was a packet of it in the gardener's shed here."

"Again very convenient," said Miss Marple. She added, "Was Mrs. Fortescue eating anything?"

"Oh, yes. They'd had tea."

"Cake, I suppose? Bread and butter? Scones, perhaps? Jam? Honey?"

"Yes, there were honey and scones, chocolate cake and swiss roll and various other plates of things." He looked at her curiously. "The potassium cyanide was in the tea, Miss Marple."

"Oh, yes, yes. I quite understand that. I was just getting the whole picture, so to speak. Rather significant, don't you think?"

He looked at her in a slightly puzzled fashion. Her cheeks were pink, her eyes were bright.

"And the third death, Inspector Neele?"

"Well, the facts there seem clear enough, too. The girl, Gladys, took in the tea tray, then she brought the next tray into the hall, but left it there. She'd been rather absentminded all the day, apparently. After that no one saw her. The cook, Mrs. Crump, jumped to the conclusion that the girl had gone out without telling anybody. She based her belief, I think, on the fact that the girl was wearing a good pair of nylon stockings and her best shoes. There, however, she was proved quite wrong. The girl had obviously remembered suddenly that she had not taken in some clothes that were drying outside on the clothesline. She ran out to fetch them in, had taken down half of them apparently, when somebody took her unawares by slipping a stocking around her neck and—well, that was that."

"Someone from outside?" said Miss Marple.

"Perhaps," said Inspector Neele. "But perhaps someone from inside. Someone who'd been waiting his or her opportunity to get the girl alone. The girl was upset, nervous, when we first questioned her, but I'm afraid we didn't quite appreciate the importance of that."

"Oh, but how could you?" cried Miss Marple. "People so often do look guilty and embarrassed when they are questioned by the police."

"That's just it. But this time, Miss Marple, it was rather more than that. I think the girl Gladys had seen someone performing some action that seemed to her needed explanation. It can't, I think, have been anything very definite. Otherwise she would have spoken out. But I think she did betray the fact to the person in question. That person realized that Gladys was a danger."

"And so Gladys was strangled and a clothes peg clipped on her nose," murmured Miss Marple to herself.

"Yes, that's a nasty touch. A nasty, sneering sort of touch. Just a nasty bit of unnecessary bravado."

Miss Marple shook her head.

"Hardly unnecessary. It does all make a pattern, doesn't it?"

Inspector Neele looked at her curiously.

"I don't quite follow you, Miss Marple. What do you mean by a pattern?"

Miss Marple immediately became flustered.

"Well, I mean it does seem—I mean, regarded as a

sequence, if you understand—well, one can't get away from facts, can one?"

"I don't think I quite understand."

"Well, I mean—first we have Mr. Fortescue. Rex Fortescue. Killed in his office in the city. And then we have Mrs. Fortescue, sitting here in the library and having tea. There were scones and honey. And then poor Gladys with the clothes peg on her nose. Just to point the whole thing. That very charming Mrs. Lance Fortescue said to me that there didn't seem to be any rhyme or reason in it, but I couldn't agree with her, because it's the rhyme that strikes one, isn't it?"

Inspector Neele said slowly, "I don't think—"

Miss Marple went on quickly, "I expect you're about thirty-five or thirty-six, aren't you, Inspector Neele? I think there was rather a reaction just then, when you were a little boy, I mean, against nursery rhymes. But if one has been brought up on Mother Goose—I mean it is really highly significant, isn't it? What I wondered was," Miss Marple paused, then appearing to take her courage in her hands, went on bravely, "Of course, it is great impertinence I know, on my part, saying this sort of thing to you."

"Please say anything you like, Miss Marple."

"Well, that's very kind of you. I shall. Though, as I say, I do it with the utmost diffidence because I know I am very old and rather muddle-headed, and I dare say my idea is of no value at all. But what I mean to say is: have you gone into the question of blackbirds?"

Chapter Fourteen

For about ten seconds Inspector Neele stared at Miss Marple with the utmost bewilderment. His first idea was that the old lady had gone off her head.

"Blackbirds?" he repeated.

Miss Marple nodded her head vigorously.

"Yes," she said, and forthwith recited,

"Sing a song of sixpence, a pocketful of rye,
Four and twenty blackbirds baked in a pie.
When the pie was opened the birds began to sing.
Wasn't that a dainty dish to set before the king?

The king was in his counting house, counting out
    his money,
The queen was in the parlour eating bread and
    honey,
The maid was in the garden hanging out the
    clothes,
When there came a little dickey bird and nipped off
    her nose."

117

"Good Lord," Inspector Neele said.

"I mean, it does fit," said Miss Marple. "It was rye in his pocket, wasn't it? One newspaper said so. The others just said cereal, which might mean anything. Farmer's Glory or Cornflakes—or even maize—but it was rye—"

Inspector Neele nodded.

"There you are," said Miss Marple, triumphantly. "Rex Fortescue. Rex means King. In his Counting House. And Mrs. Fortescue, the Queen in the parlor, eating bread and honey. And so, of course, the murderer had to put that clothes peg on poor Gladys's nose."

Inspector Neele said, "You mean the whole set up is crazy?"

"Well, one mustn't jump to conclusions, but it is certainly very odd. But you really must make inquiries about blackbirds. Because there must be blackbirds!"

It was at this point that Sergeant Hay came into the room, saying urgently, "Sir."

He broke off at the sight of Miss Marple.

Inspector Neele, recovering himself, said, "Thank you, Miss Marple. I'll look into the matter. Since you are interested in the girl, perhaps you would care to look over the things from her room. Sergeant Hay will show you them presently."

Miss Marple, accepting her dismissal, twittered her way out.

"Blackbirds!" murmured Inspector Neele to himself.

Sergeant Hay stared.

"Yes, Hay, what is it?"

"Sir," said Sergeant Hay urgently again. "Look at this."

He produced an article wrapped in a somewhat grubby handkerchief.

"Found it in the shrubbery," said Sergeant Hay.

"Could have been chucked there from one of the back windows."

He tipped the object down on the desk in front of the Inspector, who leaned forward and inspected it with rising excitement. The exhibit was a nearly full pot of marmalade.

The Inspector stared at it without speech. His face assumed a peculiarly wooden and stupid appearance. In actual fact, this meant that Inspector Neele's mind was racing once more round an imaginary track. A moving picture was enacting itself before the eyes of his mind. He saw a new pot of marmalade, he saw hands carefully removing its cover, he saw a small quantity of marmalade removed, mixed with a preparation of taxine and replaced in the pot, the top smoothed over and the lid carefully replaced.

He broke off at this point to ask Sergeant Hay, "They don't take marmalade out of the pot and put it in fancy pots?"

"No, sir. Got into the way of serving it in its own pot during the war when things were scarce, and it's gone on like that ever since."

Neele murmured, "That made it easier, of course."

"What's more," said Sergeant Hay, "Mr. Fortescue was the only one that took marmalade for breakfast (and Mr. Percival when he was at home). The others had jam or honey."

Neele nodded.

"Yes," he said. "That made it very simple, didn't it?"

After a slight gap the moving picture went on in his mind. It was the breakfast table now. Rex Fortescue stretching out his hand for the marmalade pot, taking out a spoonful of marmalade and spreading it on his toast and butter. Easier, far easier that way than the risk and difficulty of insinuating it into his coffee cup. A foolproof method of administering the poison! And afterwards? Another gap and a picture that was not quite so clear. The replacing of that pot of marmalade by another with exactly the same amount taken from it. And then an open window. A hand and an arm flinging out that pot into the shrubbery. Whose hand and arm?

Whoever had tampered with that pot of marmalade need not have been present at the breakfast table. . . .

Inspector Neele said in a business-like voice,

"Well, we'll have of course to get this analyzed. See if there are any traces of taxine. We can't jump to conclusions."

"No, sir. There may be fingerprints, too."

"Probably not the ones we want," said Inspector Neele gloomily. "There'll be Gladys's, of course, and Crump's and Fortescue's own. Then probably Mrs. Crump's, the grocer's assistant and a few others! If anyone put taxine in here, they'd take care not to go playing about with their own fingers all over the pot. Anyway, as I say, we mustn't jump to conclusions. How do they order marmalade and where is it kept?"

The industrious Sergeant Hay had his answer pat for all these questions.

"Marmalade and jams come in in batches of six at a time. A new pot would be taken into the pantry when the old one was getting low."

"That means," said Neele, "that it could have been tampered with several days before it was actually brought onto the breakfast table. And anyone who was in the house or had access to the house could have tampered with it."

The term "access to the house" puzzled Sergeant Hay slightly. He did not see in what way his superior's mind was working.

But Neele was postulating what seemed to him a logical assumption.

If the marmalade had been tampered with before-hand, then surely that ruled out those persons who were actually at the breakfast table on the fatal morning.

Which opened up some interesting new possibilities.

He planned in his mind interviews with various people—this time with rather a different angle of approach.

He'd keep an open mind. . . .

He'd even consider seriously that old Miss What's-her-name's suggestions about the nursery rhyme. Because there was no doubt that that nursery rhyme fitted in a rather startling way. It fitted with a point that had worried him from the beginning. The pocket full of rye.

"Blackbirds?" murmured Inspector Neele to himself.

Sergeant Hay stared.

"It's not blackberry jelly, sir," he said. "It's marmalade."

ii.

Inspector Neele went in search of Mary Dove.

He found her in one of the bedrooms on the first floor, superintending Ellen, who was denuding the bed of what seemed to be clean sheets. A little pile of clean towels lay on a chair.

Inspector Neele looked puzzled.

"Somebody coming to stay?" he asked.

Mary Dove smiled at him. In contrast to Ellen, who looked grim and truculent, Mary was her usual imperturbable self.

"Actually," she said, "the opposite is the case."

Neele looked inquiringly at her.

"This is the guest room we had prepared for Mr. Gerald Wright."

"Gerald Wright? Who is he?"

"He's a friend of Miss Elaine Fortescue's." Mary's voice was carefully devoid of inflection.

"He was coming here—when?"

"I believe he arrived at the Golf Hotel the day after Mr. Fortescue's death."

"The day after."

"So Miss Fortescue said." Mary's voice was still impersonal. "She told me she wanted him to come and stay in the house, so I had a room prepared. Now, after these other two—tragedies—it seems more suitable that he should remain at the hotel."

"The Golf Hotel?"

"Yes."

"Quite," said Inspector Neele.

Ellen gathered up the sheets and towels and went out of the room.

Mary Dove looked inquiringly at Neele.

"You wanted to see me about something?"

Neele said pleasantly, "It's becoming important to get exact times very clearly stated. Members of the family all seem a little vague about time—perhaps understandably. You, on the other hand, Miss Dove, I have found extremely accurate in your statements as to times."

"Again understandably!"

"Yes—perhaps—I must certainly congratulate you on the way you have kept this house going in spite of the—well, panic—these last deaths must have caused." He paused and then asked curiously: "How did you do it?"

He had realized, astutely, that the one chink in the armor of Mary Dove's inscrutability was her pleasure in her own efficiency. She unbent slightly now as she answered.

"The Crumps wanted to leave at once, of course."

"We couldn't have allowed that."

"I know. But I also told them that Mr. Percival Fortescue would be more likely to be—well—generous—to those who had spared him inconvenience."

"And Ellen?"

"Ellen does not wish to leave."

"Ellen does not wish to leave," Neele repeated. "She has good nerves."

"She enjoys disasters," said Mary Dove. "Like Mrs. Percival, she finds in disaster a kind of pleasurable drama."

"Interesting—do you think Mrs. Percival has—enjoyed the tragedies?"

"No—of course not. That is going too far. I would merely say that it has enabled her to—well—stand up to them."

"And how have you yourself been affected, Miss Dove?"

Mary Dove shrugged her shoulders.

"It has not been a pleasant experience," she said dryly.

Inspector Neele felt again a longing to break down this cool young woman's defenses—to find out what was really going on behind the careful and efficient understatement of her whole attitude.

He merely said brusquely, "Now, to recapitulate times and places: the last time you saw Gladys Martin was in the hall before tea, and that was at twenty minutes to five?"

"Yes, I told her to bring in tea."

"You yourself were coming from where?"

"From upstairs. I thought I had heard the telephone a few minutes before."

"Gladys, presumably, had answered the telephone?"

"Yes. It was a wrong number. Someone who wanted the Baydon Heath Laundry."

"And that was the last time you saw her?"

"She brought the tea tray into the library about ten minutes or so later."

"After that Miss Elaine Fortescue came in?"

"Yes, about three or four minutes later. Then I went up to tell Mrs. Percival tea was ready."

"Did you usually do that?"

"Oh, no. People came in to tea when they pleased, but Mrs. Fortescue asked where everybody was. I thought I heard Mrs. Percival coming down, but that was a mistake—"

Neele interrupted. Here was something new.

"You mean you heard someone upstairs moving about?"

"Yes, at the head of the stairs, I thought. But no one came down so I went up. Mrs. Percival was in her bedroom. She had just come in. She had been out for a walk."

"Out for a walk—I see. The time being then—"

"Oh, nearly five o'clock, I think."

"And Mr. Lancelot Fortescue arrived—when?"

"A few minutes after I came downstairs again. I thought he had arrived earlier, but—"

Inspector Neele interrupted:

"Why did you think he had arrived earlier?"

"Because I thought I had caught sight of him through the landing window."

"In the garden, you mean?"

"Yes, I caught a glimpse of someone through the yew hedge, and I thought it would probably be he."

"This was when you were coming down, after telling Mrs. Percival Fortescue tea was ready?"

Mary corrected him.

"No, not then. It was earlier—when I came down the first time."

Inspector Neele stared.

"Are you sure about that, Miss Dove?"

"Yes, I'm perfectly sure. That's why I was surprised to see him—when he actually did ring the bell."

Inspector Neele shook his head. He kept his inner excitement out of his voice as he said, "It couldn't have been Lancelot Fortescue you saw. His train—which was due at 4:28—was nine minutes late. He arrived at Baydon Heath Station at 4:37. He had to wait a few minutes for a taxi—that train is always very full. It was actually nearly a quarter to five (five minutes after you had seen the man in the garden) when he left the station and it is a ten minutes' drive. He paid off the taxi at the gate here at about five minutes to five at the earliest. No, it wasn't Lancelot Fortescue you saw."

"I'm sure I did see someone."

"Yes, you saw someone. It was getting dark. You couldn't have seen the man clearly?"

"Oh no, I couldn't see his face or anything like that—just his build—tall and slender. We were expecting Lancelot Fortescue, so I jumped to the conclusion that that's who it was."

"He was going—which way?"

"Along behind the yew hedge towards the east side of the house."

"There is a side door there. Is it kept locked?"

"Not until the house is locked up for the night."

"Anyone could have come in by that side door without being observed by any of the household."

Mary Dove considered.

"I think so. Yes." She added quickly, "You mean, the person I heard later upstairs could have come in that way? Could have been hiding—upstairs?"

"Something of the kind."

"But who—?"

"That remains to be seen. Thank you, Miss Dove."

As he turned to go away Inspector Neele said in a

casual voice, "By the way, you can't tell me anything about blackbirds, I suppose?"

For the first time, so it seemed, Mary Dove was taken aback. She turned back sharply.

"I—what did you say?"

"I was just asking you about blackbirds."

"Do you mean—"

"Blackbirds," said Inspector Neele.

He had on his most stupid expression.

"You mean that silly business last summer? But surely that can't . . ." She broke off.

Inspector Neele said pleasantly, "There's been a bit of talk about it, but I was sure I'd get a clear account from you."

Mary Dove was her calm, practical self again.

"It must, I think, have been some silly, spiteful joke," she said. "Four dead blackbirds were on Mr. Fortescue's desk in his study here. It was summer and the windows were open, and we rather thought it must have been the gardener's boy, though he insisted he'd never done anything of the kind. But they were actually blackbirds the gardener had shot, which had been hanging up by the fruit bushes."

"And somebody had cut them down and put them on Mr. Fortescue's desk?"

"Yes."

"Any sort of reason behind it—any association with blackbirds?"

Mary shook her head.

"I don't think so."

"How did Mr. Fortescue take it? Was he annoyed?"

"Naturally he was annoyed."

"But not upset in any way?"

"I really can't remember."

"I see," said Inspector Neele.

He said no more. Mary Dove once more turned away,

but this time, he thought, she went rather unwillingly, as though she would have liked to know more of what was in his mind. Ungratefully, all that Inspector Neele felt was annoyance with Miss Marple. She had suggested to him that there would be blackbirds and sure enough, there the blackbirds were! Not four and twenty of them, that was true. What might be called a token consignment.

That had been as long ago as last summer, and where it fitted in Inspector Neele could not imagine. He was not going to let this blackbird bogy divert him from the logical and sober investigation of murder by a sane murderer for a sane reason, but he would be forced from now on to keep the crazier possibilities of the case in mind.

Chapter Fifteen

"I'm sorry, Miss Fortescue, to bother you again, but I want to be quite, quite clear about this. As far as we know you were the last person—or rather the last person but one—to see Mrs. Fortescue alive. It was about twenty past five when you left the drawing-room?"

"About then," said Elaine, "I can't say exactly." She added defensively, "One doesn't look at clocks the whole time."

"No, of course not. During the time that you were alone with Mrs. Fortescue after the others had left, what did you talk about?"

"Does it matter what we talked about?"

"Probably not," said Inspector Neele, "but it might give me some clue as to what was in Mrs. Fortescue's mind."

"You mean—you think she might have done it herself?"

Inspector Neele noticed the brightening of her face. It would certainly be a very convenient solution as far as the family was concerned. Inspector Neele did not think it was true for a moment. Adele Fortescue was not, to his mind, a suicidal type. Even if she had poisoned her husband and was convinced the crime was about to be brought home to her, she would not, he thought, have ever thought of killing herself. She would have been optimistically sure that even if she were tried for murder she would be sure to be acquitted. He was not, however, averse to Elaine Fortescue's entertaining the hypothesis. He said, therefore, quite truthfully,

"There's a possibility of it, at least, Miss Fortescue. Now perhaps you'll tell me just what your conversation was about."

"Well, it was really about my affairs." Elaine hesitated.

"Your affairs being . . . ?" He paused questioningly with a general expression.

"I—a friend of mine had just arrived in the neighborhood, and I was asking Adele if she would have any objection to—to my asking him to stay here at the house."

"Ah. And who is this friend?"

"It's a Mr. Gerald Wright. He's a schoolmaster. He—he's staying at the Golf Hotel."

"A very close friend, perhaps?"

Inspector Neele gave an avuncular beam which added at least fifteen years to his age.

"We may expect an interesting announcement shortly, perhaps?"

He felt almost compunction as he saw the awkward gesture of the girl's hand and the flush on her face. She was in love with the fellow all right.

"We—we're not actually engaged and of course we

couldn't have it announced just now, but—well, yes, I think we do—I mean we are going to get married."

"Congratulations," said Inspector Neele pleasantly. "Mr. Wright is staying at the Golf Hotel, isn't he? How long has he been there?"

"I wired him when Father died."

."And he came at once. I see," said Inspector Neele. He used this favorite phrase of his in a friendly and reassuring way.

"What did Mrs. Fortescue say when you asked her about his coming here?"

"Oh, she said, all right, I could have anybody I pleased."

"She was nice about it then?"

"Not exactly nice. I mean she said—"

"Yes, what else did she say?"

Again Elaine flushed.

"Oh, something stupid about my being able to do a lot better for myself now. It was the sort of thing Adele would say."

"Ah, well," said Inspector Neele soothingly, "relations say these sort of things."

"Yes, yes, they do. But people often find it difficult to—to appreciate Gerald properly. He's an intellectual, you see, and he's got a lot of unconventional and progressive ideas that people don't like."

"That's why he didn't get on with your father?"

Elaine flushed hotly.

"Father was very prejudiced and unjust. He hurt Gerald's feelings. In fact, Gerald was so upset by my father's attitude that he went off and I didn't hear from him for weeks."

And probably wouldn't have heard from him now if your father hadn't died and left you a packet of money, Inspector Neele thought. Aloud he said, "Was there any more conversation between you and Mrs. Fortescue?"

"No. No, I don't think so."

"And that was about twenty-five past five, and Mrs. Fortescue was found dead at five minutes to six. You didn't return to the room during that half hour?"

"No."

"What were you doing?"

"I—I went out for a short walk."

"To the Golf Hotel?"

"I—well, yes, but Gerald wasn't in."

Inspector Neele said "I see" again, but this time with a rather dismissive effect.

Elaine Fortescue got up and said, "Is that all?"

"That's all, thank you, Miss Fortescue."

As she got up to go, Neele said casually, "You can't tell me anything about blackbirds, can you?"

She stared at him.

"Blackbirds? You mean the ones in the pie?"

They would be in the pie, the Inspector thought to himself. He merely said, "When was this?"

"Oh, three or four months ago—and there were some on Father's desk, too. He was furious."

"Furious, was he? Did he ask a lot of questions?"

"Yes, of course. But we couldn't find out who put them there."

"Have you any idea why he was so angry?"

"Well, it was rather a horrid thing to do, wasn't it?"

Neele looked thoughtfully at her, but he did not see any signs of evasion in her face. He said, "Oh, just one more thing, Miss Fortescue. Do you know if your stepmother made a will at any time?"

Elaine shook her head.

"I've no idea. I suppose so. People usually do, don't they?"

"They should do, but it doesn't always follow. Have you made a will yourself, Miss Fortescue?"

"No—no—I haven't—up to now I haven't had anything to leave. Now, of course—"

He saw the realization of the changed position come
into her eyes.

"Yes," he said. "Fifty thousand pounds is quite a
responsibility. It changes a lot of things, Miss Fortescue."

ii.

For some minutes after Elaine Fortescue left the
room, Inspector Neele sat staring in front of him
thoughtfully. He had, indeed, new food for thought.
Mary Dove's statement that she had seen a man in the
garden at approximately 4:35 opened up certain new
possibilities. That is, of course, if Mary Dove was
speaking the truth. It was never Inspector Neele's habit
to assume that anyone was speaking the truth. But,
examine her statement as he might, he could see no real
reason why she should have lied. He was inclined to
think that Mary Dove was speaking the truth when she
spoke of having seen a man in the garden. It was quite
clear that that man could not have been Lancelot Fortescue, although her reason for assuming that it was he
was quite natural under the circumstances. It had not
been Lancelot Fortescue, but it had been a man about
the height and build of Lancelot Fortescue, and if
there had been a man in the garden at that particular
time, moreover a man moving furtively, as it seemed,
to judge from the way he had crept behind the yew
hedges, then that certainly opened up a line of thought.

Added to this statement of hers, there had been the
further statement that she had heard someone moving
about upstairs. That, in its turn, tied up with something
else. The small piece of mud he had found on the floor

of Adele Fortescue's boudoir. Inspector Neele's mind dwelt on the small dainty desk in that room. Pretty little sham antique with a rather obvious secret drawer in it. There had been three letters in that drawer, letters written by Vivian Dubois to Adele Fortescue. A great many love letters of one kind or another had passed through Inspector Neele's hands in the course of his career. He was acquainted with passionate letters, foolish letters, sentimental letters and nagging letters. There had also been cautious letters. Inspector Neele was inclined to classify these three as of the latter kind. Even if read in the divorce court, they could pass as inspired by a merely platonic friendship. Though in this case— "Platonic friendship, my foot!" thought the Inspector inelegantly.

Neele, when he had found the letters, had sent them up at once to the Yard since, at that time, the main question was whether the Public Prosecutor's office thought that there was sufficient evidence to proceed with the case against Adele Fortescue or Adele Fortescue and Vivian Dubois together. Everything had pointed towards Rex Fortescue having been poisoned by his wife with or without her lover's connivance. These letters, though cautious, made it fairly clear that Vivian Dubois was her lover, but there had not been in the wording, so far as Inspector Neele could see, any signs of incitement to crime. There might have been incitement of a spoken kind, but Vivian Dubois would be far too cautious to put anything of that kind down on paper.

Inspector Neele surmised accurately that Vivian Dubois had asked Adele Fortescue to destroy his letters and that Adele Fortescue had told him she had done so.

Well, now they had two more deaths on their hands. And that meant, or should mean, that Adele Fortescue had not killed her husband.

Unless, that is—Inspector Neele considered a new hypothesis. Adele Fortescue had wanted to marry Vivian Dubois and Vivian Dubois had wanted, not Adele Fortescue, but Adele Fortescue's hundred thousand pounds which would come to her on the death of her husband. He had assumed, perhaps, that Rex Fortescue's death would be put down to natural causes. Some kind of seizure or stroke. After all, everybody seemed to be worried over Rex Fortescue's health during the last year. (Parenthetically, Inspector Neele said to himself that he must look into that question. He had a subconscious feeling that it might be important in some way.) To continue: Rex Fortescue's death had not gone according to plan. It had been diagnosed, without loss of time, as poisoning and the correct poison named.

Supposing that Adele Fortescue and Vivian Dubois had been guilty, what state would they be in then? Vivian Dubois would have been scared and Adele Fortescue would have lost her head. She might have done or said foolish things. She might have rung up Dubois on the telephone, talking indiscreetly in a way that he would have realized might have been overheard in Yew-tree Lodge. What would Vivian Dubois have done next?

It was early as yet to try and answer that question, but Inspector Neele proposed very shortly to make inquiries at the Golf Hotel as to whether Dubois had been in or out of the hotel between the hours of 4:15 and 6 o'clock. Vivian Dubois was tall and dark like Lance Fortescue. He might have slipped through the garden to the side door, made his way upstairs, and then what? Looked for the letters and found them gone? Waited there, perhaps, till the coast was clear, then come down into the library when tea was over and Adele Fortescue was alone?

But all this was going too fast—

Neele had questioned Mary Dove and Elaine Fortescue; he must see now what Percival Fortescue's wife had to say.

Chapter Sixteen

Inspector Neele found Mrs. Percival in her own sitting room upstairs, writing letters. She got up rather nervously when he came in.

"Is there anything—what—are there—"

"Please sit down, Mrs. Fortescue. There are only just a few more questions I would like to ask you."

"Oh, yes. Yes, of course, Inspector. It's all so dreadful, isn't it? So very dreadful."

She sat down rather nervously in an armchair. Inspector Neele sat down in the small, straight chair near her. He studied her rather more carefully than he had done heretofore. In some ways a mediocre type of woman, he thought—and thought also that she was not very happy. Restless, unsatisfied, limited in mental outlook, yet he thought she might have been efficient and skilled in her own profession of hospital nurse. Though she had achieved leisure by her marriage with a well-to-do man, leisure had not satisfied her. She bought clothes, read novels and ate sweets, but he remembered her avid excitement on the night of Rex Fortescue's death, and he saw in it not so much a ghoulish satisfaction but rather a revelation of the arid deserts of boredom which encompassed her life. Her eyelids fluttered and fell before his searching glance. They gave her the appearance of being both nervous and guilty, but he could not be sure that that was really the case.

"I'm afraid," he said soothingly, "we have to ask people questions again and again. It must be very tiresome for you all. I do appreciate that, but so much hangs, you understand, on the exact timing of events. You came down to tea rather late, I understand? In fact, Miss Dove came up and fetched you."

"Yes. Yes, she did. She came in and said tea was in. I had no idea it was so late. I'd been writing letters."

Inspector Neele just glanced over at the writing desk.

"I see," he said. "Somehow, or other, I thought you'd been out for a walk."

"Did she say so? Yes, now I believe you're right. I had been writing letters; then it was so stuffy and my head ached so I went out and—er—went for a walk. Only round the garden."

"I see. You didn't meet anyone?"

"Meet anyone?" She stared at him. "What do you mean?"

"Just wondered if you'd seen anybody or anybody had seen you during this walk of yours."

"I saw the gardener in the distance, that's all." She was looking at him suspiciously.

"Then you came in, came up here to your room and you were just taking your things off when Miss Dove came to tell you that tea was ready?"

"Yes. Yes, and so I came down."

"And who was there?"

"Adele and Elaine, and a minute or two later Lance

arrived. My brother-in-law, you know. The one who's
back from Kenya."

"And then you all had tea?"

"Yes, we had tea. Then Lance went up to see Aunt
Effie and I came up here to finish my letters. I left
Elaine there with Adele."

He nodded reassuringly.

"Yes. Miss Fortescue seems to have been with Mrs.
Fortescue for quite five or ten minutes after you left.
Your husband hadn't come home yet?"

"Oh no. Percy—Val—didn't get home until about
half-past six or seven. He'd been kept up in town."

"He came by train?"

"Yes. He took a taxi from the station."

"Was it unusual for him to come back by train?"

"He does sometimes. Not very often. I think he'd
been to places in the city where it's rather difficult to
park the car. It was easier for him to take a train home
from Cannon Street."

"I see," said Inspector Neele. He went on, "I asked
your husband if Mrs. Fortescue had made a will before
she died. He said he thought not. I suppose you don't
happen to have any idea?"

To his surprise Jennifer Fortescue nodded vigorously.

"Oh, yes," she said. "Adele made a will. She told me
so."

"Indeed! When was this?"

"Oh, it wasn't very long ago. About a month ago, I
think."

"That's very interesting," said Inspector Neele.

Mrs. Percival leant forward eagerly. Her face now
was all animation. She clearly enjoyed exhibiting her
superior knowledge.

"Val didn't know about it," she said. "Nobody knew.
It just happened that I found out about it. I was in the
street. I had just come out of the stationer's; then I saw

Adele coming out of the solicitor's office. Ansell and Worrall's, you know. In the High Street."

"Ah," said Neele, "the local solicitors?"

"Yes. And I said to Adele, 'Whatever have you been doing there?' And she laughed and said, 'Wouldn't you like to know?' And then as we walked along together she said, 'I'll tell you, Jennifer. I've been making my will.' 'Well,' I said. 'Why are you doing that, Adele? You're not ill or anything, are you?' And she said no, of course she wasn't ill. She'd never felt better. But everyone ought to make a will. She said she wasn't going to those stuck-up family solicitors in London, Mr. Billingsley. She said the old sneak would go round and tell the family. 'No,' she said. 'My will's my own business, Jennifer, and I'll make it my own way and nobody's going to know about it.' 'Well, Adele,' I said, 'I shan't tell anybody.' She said, "It doesn't matter if you do. You won't know what's in it.' But I didn't tell anyone. No, not even Percy. I do think women ought to stick together, don't you, Inspector Neele?"

"I'm sure that's a very nice feeling on your part, Mrs. Fortescue," said Inspector Neele diplomatically.

"I'm sure I'm never ill-natured," said Jennifer. "I didn't particularly care for Adele, if you know what I mean. I always thought she was the kind of woman who would stick at nothing in order to get what she wanted. Now she's dead, perhaps I misjudged her, poor soul."

"Well, thank you very much, Mrs. Fortescue, for being so helpful to me."

"You're welcome, I'm sure. I'm only too glad to do anything I can. It's all so very terrible, isn't it? Who is the old lady who's arrived this morning?"

"She's a Miss Marple. She very kindly came here to give us what information she could about the girl Gladys. It seems Gladys Martin was once in service with her."

"Really? How interesting."

"There's one other thing, Mrs. Percival. Do you know anything about blackbirds?"

Jennifer Fortescue started violently. She dropped her handbag on the floor and bent to pick it up.

"Blackbirds, Inspector? Blackbirds? What kind of blackbirds?" Her voice was rather breathless.

Smiling a little, Inspector Neele said, "Just blackbirds. Alive or dead or even, shall we say, symbolical?"

Jennifer Fortescue said sharply, "I don't know what you mean. I don't know what you're talking about."

"You don't know anything about blackbirds, then, Mrs. Fortescue?"

She said slowly, "I suppose you mean the ones last summer in the pie. All very silly."

"There were some left on the library table, too, weren't there?"

"It was all a very silly practical joke. I don't know who's been talking to you about it. Mr. Fortescue, my father-in-law, was very much annoyed by it."

"Just annoyed? Nothing more?"

"Oh, I see what you mean. Yes, I suppose—yes, it's true. He asked us if there were any strangers about the place."

"Strangers!" Inspector Neele raised his eyebrows.

"Well, that's what he said," said Mrs. Percival defensively.

"Strangers," repeated Inspector Neele thoughtfully. Then he asked, "Did he seem afraid in any way?"

"Afraid? I don't know what you mean."

"Nervous. About strangers, I mean."

"Yes. Yes, he did, rather. Of course, I don't remember very well. It was several months ago, you know. I don't think it was anything except a silly practical joke. Crump perhaps. I really do think that Crump is a very unbalanced man, and I'm perfectly certain that he

drinks. He's really very insolent in his manner sometimes. I've sometimes wondered if he could have had a
grudge against Mr. Fortescue. Do you think that's possible, Inspector?"

"Anything's possible," said Inspector Neele and went
away.

ii.

Percival Fortescue was in London, but Inspector Neele
found Lancelot sitting with his wife in the library. They
were playing chess together.

"I don't want to interrupt you," said Neele apologetically.

"We're only killing time, Inspector, aren't we, Pat?"

Pat nodded.

"I expect you'll think it's rather a foolish question
I'm asking you," said Neele. "Do you know anything
about blackbirds, Mr. Fortescue?"

"Blackbirds?" Lance looked amused. "What kind of
blackbirds? Do you mean genuine birds, or the slave
trade?"

Inspector Neele said with a sudden, disarming smile,
"I'm not sure what I mean, Mr. Fortescue. It's just that
a mention of blackbirds has turned up."

"Good Lord." Lancelot looked suddenly alert. "Not
the old Blackbird Mine, I suppose?"

Inspector Neele said sharply,

"The Blackbird Mine? What was that?"

Lance frowned in a puzzled fashion.

"The trouble is, Inspector, that I can't really remember much myself. I just have a vague idea about some
shady transaction in my papa's past. Something on the
West Coast of Africa. Aunt Effie, I believe, once threw
it in his teeth, but I can't remember anything definite
about it."

"Aunt Effie? That will be Miss Ramsbottom, won't it?"

"Yes."

"I'll go and ask her about it," said Inspector Neele. He added ruefully, "She's rather a formidable old lady, Mr. Fortescue. Always makes me feel quite nervous."

Lance laughed.

"Yes. Aunt Effie is certainly a character, but she may be helpful to you, Inspector, if you get on the right side of her. Especially if you're delving into the past. She's got an excellent memory; she takes a positive pleasure in remembering anything that's detrimental in any way." He added thoughtfully, "There's something else. I went up to see her, you know, soon after I got back here. Immediately after tea that day, as a matter of fact. And she was talking about Gladys. The maid who got killed. Not that we knew she was dead then, of course. But Aunt Effie was saying she was quite convinced that Gladys knew something that she hadn't told the police."

"That seems fairly certain," said Inspector Neele. "She'll never tell it now, poor girl."

"No. It seems Aunt Effie had given her good advice as to spilling anything she knew. Pity the girl didn't take it."

Inspector Neele nodded. Bracing himself for the encounter, he penetrated to Miss Ramsbottom's fortress. Rather to his surprise, he found Miss Marple there. The two ladies appeared to be discussing foreign missions.

"I'll go away, Inspector." Miss Marple rose hurriedly to her feet.

"No need, madam," said Inspector Neele.

"I've asked Miss Marple to come and stay in the house," said Miss Ramsbottom. "No sense in spending money in that ridiculous Golf Hotel. A wicked nest of profiteers, that is. Drinking and card-playing all the evening. She'd better come and stay in a decent Christian

household. There's a room next door to mine. Dr. Mary
Peters, the missionary, had it last."

"It's very, very kind of you," said Miss Marple, "but
I really think I mustn't intrude in a house of mourning."

"Mourning? Fiddlesticks," said Miss Ramsbottom.
"Who'll weep for Rex in this house? Or Adele either?
Or is it the police you're worried about? Any objections,
Inspector?"

"None from me, madam."

"There you are," said Miss Ramsbottom.

"It's very kind of you," said Miss Marple gratefully.
"I'll go and telephone to the hotel to cancel my book-
ing." She left the room.

Miss Ramsbottom said sharply to the Inspector,
"Well, and what do you want?"

"I wondered if you could tell me anything about the
Blackbird Mine, ma'am."

Miss Ramsbottom uttered a sudden, shrill cackle of
laughter.

"Ha. You've got on to that, have you! Took the hint
I gave you the other day. Well, what do you want to
know about it?"

"Anything you can tell me, madam."

"I can't tell you much. It's a long time ago now—
oh, twenty to twenty-five years, maybe. Some concession or other in East Africa. My brother-in-law went
into it with a man called MacKenzie. They went out
there to investigate the mine together, and MacKenzie
died out there of fever. Rex came home and said the
claim or the concession or whatever you call it was
worthless. That's all I know."

"I think you know a little more than that, ma'am,"
said Neele persuasively.

"Anything else is hearsay. You don't like hearsay in
the law, so I've been told."

"We're not in court yet, ma'am."

"Well, I can't tell you anything. The MacKenzies kicked up a fuss. That's all I know. They insisted that Rex had swindled MacKenzie. I daresay he did. He was a clever, unscrupulous fellow, but I've no doubt whatever he did it was all legal. They couldn't prove anything. Mrs. MacKenzie was an unbalanced sort of woman. She came here and made a lot of threats of revenge. Said Rex had murdered her husband. Silly, melodramatic fuss! I think she was a bit off her head—in fact, I believe she went into an asylum not long after. Came here dragging along a couple of young children who looked scared to death. Said she'd bring up her children to have revenge. Something like that. Tomfoolery, all of it. Well, that's all I can tell you. And mind you, the Blackbird Mine wasn't the only swindle that Rex put over in his lifetime. You'll find a good many more if you look for them. What put you on the Blackbird? Did you come across some trail leading to the MacKenzies?"

"You don't know what became of the family, ma'am?"

"No idea," said Miss Ramsbottom. "Mind you, I don't think Rex would have actually murdered Mac-Kenzie, but he might have left him to die. The same thing before the Lord, but not the same thing before the law. If he did, retribution's caught up with him. The mills of God grind slowly, but they grind exceedingly small. You'd better go away now. I can't tell you any more and it's no good your asking."

"Thank you very much for what you have told me," said Inspector Neele.

"Send that Marple woman back," Miss Ramsbottom called after him. "She's frivolous, like all Church of England people, but she knows how to run a charity in a sensible way."

Inspector Neele made a couple of telephone calls,

the first to Ansell and Worrall and the second to the Golf Hotel. Then he summoned Sergeant Hay and told him that he was leaving the house for a short period.

"I've a short call to pay at a solicitor's office; after that, you can get me at the Golf Hotel if anything urgent turns up."

"Yes, sir."

"And find out anything you can about blackbirds," added Neele over his shoulder.

"Blackbirds, sir?" Sergeant Hay repeated, thoroughly mystified.

"That's what I said—not blackberry jelly—blackbirds."

"Very good, sir," said Sergeant Hay bewilderedly.

Chapter Seventeen

Inspector Neele found Mr. Ansell the type of solicitor who was more easily intimidated than intimidating. A member of a small and not very prosperous firm, he was anxious not to stand upon his rights but instead to assist the police in every way possible.

Yes, he said, he had made a will for the late Mrs. Adele Fortescue. She had called at his office about five weeks previously. It had seemed to him rather a peculiar business, but naturally he had not said anything. Peculiar things did happen in a solicitor's business, and of course the Inspector would understand that discretion, etc., etc. The Inspector nodded to show he understood. He had already discovered Mr. Ansell had not transacted any legal business previously for Mrs. Fortescue or for any of the Fortescue family.

"Naturally," said Mr. Ansell, "she didn't want to go to her husband's firm of lawyers about this."

Shorn of verbiage, the facts were simple. Adele Fortescue had made a will leaving everything of which she died possessed to Vivian Dubois.

"But I gathered," said Mr. Ansell, looking at Neele in an interrogating manner, "that she hadn't actually much to leave."

Inspector Neele nodded. At the time Adele Fortescue made her will that was true enough. But since then Rex Fortescue had died, and Adele Fortescue had inherited £100,000 and presumably that £100,000 (less death duties) now belonged to Vivian Edward Dubois.

ii.

At the Golf Hotel, Inspector Neele found Vivian Dubois nervously awaiting his arrival. Dubois had been on the point of leaving, indeed his bags were packed, when he had received over the telephone a civil request from Inspector Neele to remain. Inspector Neele had been very pleasant about it, quite apologetic. But behind the conventional words the request had been an order. Vivian Dubois had demurred, but not too much.

He said now, "I do hope you realize, Inspector Neele, that it is very inconvenient for me to have to stay on. I really have urgent business that needs attending to."

"I didn't know you were in business, Mr. Dubois," said Inspector Neele genially.

"I'm afraid none of us can be as leisured as we would like to appear to be nowadays."

"Mrs. Fortescue's death must have been a great shock to you, Mr. Dubois. You were great friends, were you not?"

"Yes," said Dubois. "She was a charming woman. We played golf quite often together."

"I expect you'll miss her very much."

"Yes, indeed." Dubois sighed. "The whole thing is really quite, quite terrible."

"You actually telephoned her, I believe, on the afternoon of her death?"

"Did I? I really cannot remember now."

"About four o'clock, I understand."

"Yes, I believe I did."

"Don't you remember what your conversation was about, Mr. Dubois?"

"It wasn't of any significance. I think I asked her how she was feeling and if there was any further news about her husband's death—a more or less conventional inquiry."

"I see," said Inspector Neele. He added, "And then you went out for a walk?"

"Eh—yes—yes, I—I did, I think. At least, not a walk, I played a few holes of golf."

Inspector Neele said gently, "I think not, Mr. Dubois. . . . Not that particular day. . . . The porter here noticed you walking down the road towards Yewtree Lodge."

Dubois' eyes met his, then shied away again nervously.

"I'm afraid I can't remember, Inspector."

"Perhaps you actually went to call upon Mrs. Fortescue?"

Dubois said sharply, "No. No, I didn't do that. I never went near the house."

"Where did you go, then?"

"Oh, I—went on down the road, down as far as the Three Pigeons and then I turned around and came back by the links."

"You're quite sure you didn't go to Yewtree Lodge?"

"Quite sure, Inspector."

The Inspector shook his head.

"Come, now, Mr. Dubois," he said, "it's much better to be frank with us, you know. You may have had some quite innocent reason for going there."

"I tell you I never went up to see Mrs. Fortescue that day."

The Inspector stood up.

"You know, Mr. Dubois," he said pleasantly, "I think we'll have to ask you for a statement and you'll be well advised and quite within your rights in having a solicitor present when you are making your statement."

The color fled from Mr. Dubois' face, leaving it a sickly greenish color.

"You're threatening me," he said. "You're threatening me."

"No, no, nothing of the kind." Inspector Neele spoke in a shocked voice. "We're not allowed to do anything of that sort. Quite the contrary. I'm actually pointing out to you that you have certain rights."

"I had nothing to do with it all, I tell you! Nothing to do with it."

"Come now, Mr. Dubois, you were at Yewtree Lodge round half-past four on that day. Somebody looked out of the window, you know, and saw you."

"I was only in the garden. I didn't go into the house."

"Didn't you?" said Inspector Neele. "Are you sure? Didn't you go in by the side door, and up the stairs to Mrs. Fortescue's sitting-room on the first floor? You were looking for something, weren't you, in the desk there?"

"You've got them, I suppose," said Dubois sullenly. "That fool Adele kept them, then she swore she burnt them. But they don't mean what you think they mean."

"You're not denying, are you, Mr. Dubois, that you were a very close friend of Mrs. Fortescue's?"

"No, of course I'm not. How can I when you've got the letters? All I say is, there's no need to go reading any sinister meaning into them. Don't think for a moment that we—that she—ever thought of getting rid of Rex Fortescue. Good God, I'm not that kind of man!"

"But perhaps she was that kind of woman?"

"Nonsense," cried Vivian Dubois, "wasn't she killed, too?"

"Oh yes, yes."

"Well, isn't it natural to believe that the same person who killed her husband killed her?"

"It might be. It certainly might be. But there are other solutions. For instance (this is quite a hypothetical case, Mr. Dubois), it's possible that Mrs. Fortescue got rid of her husband, and that after his death she became somewhat of a danger to someone else. Someone who had, perhaps, not helped her in what she had done but who had at least encouraged her and provided, shall we say, the motive for the deed. She might be, you know, a danger to that particular person."

Dubois stammered, "You c-c-can't build up a case against me. You can't."

"She made a will, you know," said Inspector Neele. "She left all her money to you. Everything she possessed."

"I don't want the money. I don't want a penny of it."

"Of course, it isn't very much really," said Inspector Neele. "There's jewelry and some furs, but I imagine very little actual cash."

Dubois stared at him, his jaw dropping.

"But I thought her husband—"

He stopped dead.

"Did you, Mr. Dubois?" said Inspector Neele, and there was steel now in his voice. "That's very interesting. I wondered if you knew the terms of Rex Fortescue's will."

iii.

Inspector Neele's second interview at the Golf Hotel was with Mr. Gerald Wright. Mr. Gerald Wright was a thin, intellectual and very superior young man. He was, Inspector Neele noted, not unlike Vivian Dubois in build.

"What can I do for you, Inspector Neele?" he asked.

"I thought you might be able to help us with a little information, Mr. Wright."

"Information? Really? It seems very unlikely."

"It's in connection with the recent events at Yewtree Lodge. You've heard of them, of course?"

Inspector Neele put a little irony into the question. Mr. Wright smiled patronizingly.

"Heard of them," he said, "is hardly the right word. The newspapers appear to be full of nothing else. How incredibly bloodthirsty our public press is! What an age we live in! On one side the manufacture of atom bombs, on the other our newspapers delight in reporting brutal murders! But you said you had some questions to ask. Really, I cannot see what they can be. I know nothing about this Yewtree Lodge affair. I was actually in the Isle of Man when Mr. Fortescue was killed."

"You arrived here very shortly afterwards, didn't you, Mr. Wright? You had a telegram, I believe, from Miss Elaine Fortescue."

"Our police know everything, do they not? Yes, Elaine sent for me. I came, of course, at once."

"And you are, I understand, shortly to be married?"

"Quite right, Inspector Neele. You have no objections, I hope."

"It is entirely Miss Fortescue's business. I understand the attachment between you dates from some time back? Six or seven months ago, in fact?"

"Quite correct."

"You and Miss Fortescue became engaged to be married, but Mr. Fortescue refused to give his consent and informed you that if his daughter married against his wishes he did not propose to give her an income of any kind. Whereupon, I understand, you broke off the engagement and departed."

Gerald Wright smiled rather pityingly.

"A very crude way of putting things, Inspector Neele. Actually, I was victimized for my political opinions. Rex Fortescue was the worst type of capitalist. Naturally, I could not sacrifice my political beliefs and convictions for money."

"But you have no objections to marrying a wife who has just inherited £50,000?"

Gerald Wright gave a thin, satisfied smile.

"Not at all, Inspector Neele. The money will be used for the benefit of the community. But surely you did not come here to discuss with me either my financial circumstances—or my political convictions?"

"No, Mr. Wright. I wanted to talk to you about a simple question of fact. As you are aware, Mrs. Adele Fortescue died as a result of cyanide poisoning on the afternoon of November first. Since you were in the neighborhood of Yewtree Lodge on that afternoon I thought it possible that you might have seen or heard something that had a bearing on the case."

"And what leads you to believe that I was, as you call it, in the neighborhood of Yewtree Lodge at the time?"

"You left this hotel at a quarter-past four on that particular afternoon, Mr. Wright. On leaving the hotel you walked down the road in the direction of Yewtree Lodge. It seems natural to suppose that you were going there."

"I thought of it," said Gerald Wright, "but I considered that it would be a rather pointless thing to do. I already had an arrangement to meet Miss Fortescue—Elaine—at the hotel at six o'clock. I went for a walk along a lane that branches off from the main road and returned to the Golf Hotel just before six o'clock.

Elaine did not keep her appointment. Quite naturally, under the circumstances."

"Anybody see you on this walk of yours, Mr. Wright?"

"A few cars passed me, I think, on the road. I did not see anyone I know, if that's what you mean. The lane was little more than a cart track and too muddy for cars."

"So, between the time you left the hotel at a quarter-past four until six o'clock when you arrived back again, I've only your word for it as to where you were?"

Gerald Wright continued to smile in a superior fashion.

"Very distressing for us both, Inspector, but there it is."

Inspector Neele said softly, "Then if someone said they looked out of a landing window and saw you in the garden of Yewtree Lodge at about 4:35—" He paused and left the sentence unfinished.

Gerald Wright raised his eyebrows and shook his head.

"Visibility must have been very bad by then," he said. "I think it would be difficult for anyone to be sure."

"Are you acquainted with Mr. Vivian Dubois, who is also staying here?"

"Dubois. Dubois? No, I don't think so. Is that the tall, dark man with a pretty taste in suede shoes?"

"Yes. He also was out for a walk that afternoon, and he also left the hotel and walked past Yewtree Lodge. You did not notice him in the road by any chance?"

"No. No. I can't say I did."

Gerald Wright looked for the first time faintly worried.

Inspector Neele said thoughtfully, "It wasn't really a very nice afternoon for walking, especially after dark in a muddy lane. Curious how energetic everyone seems to have felt."

iv.

On Inspector Neele's return to the house he was greeted by Sergeant Hay with an air of satisfaction.

"I've found out about the blackbirds for you, sir," he said.

"You have, have you?"

"Yes, sir, in a pie they were. Cold pie was left out for Sunday night's supper. Somebody got at that pie in the larder or somewhere. They'd taken off the crust and they'd taken out the veal and 'am what was inside it, and what d'you think they put in, instead? Some stinkin' blackbirds they got out of the gardener's shed. Nasty sort of trick to play, wasn't it?"

" *'Wasn't that a dainty dish to set before the king?'* " said Inspector Neele.

He left Sergeant Hay staring after him.

Chapter Eighteen

"Just wait a minute," said Miss Ramsbottom. "This patience is going to come out."

She transferred a king and his various impedimenta into an empty space, put a red seven on a black eight, built up the four, five and six of spades on her foundation heap, made a few more rapid transfers of cards and then leaned back with a sigh of satisfaction.

"That's the double jester," she said. "It doesn't often come out."

She leaned back in a satisfied fashion, then raised her eyes at the girl standing by the fireplace.

"So you're Lance's wife," she said.

Pat, who had been summoned upstairs to Miss Ramsbottom's presence, nodded her head.

"Yes," she said.

"You're a tall girl," said Miss Ramsbottom, "and you look healthy."

"I'm very healthy."

Miss Ramsbottom nodded in a satisfied manner.

"Percival's wife is pasty," she said. "Eats too many sweets and doesn't take enough exercise. Well, sit down, child, sit down. Where did you meet my nephew?"

"I met him out in Kenya when I was staying there with some friends."

"You've been married before, I understand."

"Yes. Twice."

Miss Ramsbottom gave a profound sniff.

"Divorce, I suppose."

"No," said Pat. Her voice trembled a little. "They both—died. My first husband was a fighter pilot. He was killed in the war."

"And your second husband? Let me see—somebody told me. Shot himself, didn't he?"

Pat nodded.

"Your fault?"

"No," said Pat. "It wasn't my fault."

"Racing man, wasn't he?"

"Yes."

"I've never been on a race course in my life," said Miss Ramsbottom. "Betting and card-playing—all devices of the devil!"

Pat did not reply.

"I wouldn't go inside a theater or a cinema," said Miss Ramsbottom. "Ah, well, it's a wicked world nowadays. A lot of wickedness was going on in the house, but the Lord struck them down."

Pat still found it difficult to say anything. She wondered if Lance's Aunt Effie was really quite all there. She was, however, a trifle disconcerted by the old lady's shrewd glance at her.

"How much," demanded Aunt Effie, "do you know about the family you've married into?"

"I suppose," said Pat, "as much as one ever knows of the family one marries into."

"H'm, something in that, something in that. Well, I'll tell you this. My sister was a fool, my brother-in-law was a rogue, Percival is a sneak, and your Lance was always the bad boy of the family."

"I think that's all nonsense," said Pat robustly.

"Maybe you're right," said Miss Ramsbottom unexpectedly. "You can't just stick labels on people. But don't underestimate Percival. There's a tendency to believe that those who are labeled good are also stupid. Percival isn't the least bit stupid. He's quite clever in a sanctimonious kind of way. I've never cared for him. Mind you, I don't trust Lance and I don't approve of him, but I can't help being fond of him. . . . He's a reckless sort of fellow—always has been. You've got to look after him and see he doesn't go too far. Tell him not to underestimate Percival, my dear. Tell him not to believe everything that Percival says. They're all liars in this house." The old lady added with satisfaction, "Fire and brimstone shall be their portion."

ii.

Inspector Neele was finishing a telephone conversation with Scotland Yard.

The Assistant Commissioner at the other end said, "We ought to be able to get that information for you— by circularizing the various private sanatoriums. Of course, she may be dead."

"Probably is. It's a long time ago."

Old sins cast long shadows. Miss Ramsbottom had said that—said it with significance, too, as though she was giving him a hint.

"It's a fantastic theory," said the A.C.

"Don't I know it, sir. But I don't feel we can ignore it altogether. Too much fits in."

"Yes—yes—rye—blackbirds—the man's Christian name."

Neele said, "I'm concentrating on the other lines too. Dubois is a possibility. So is Wright. The girl Gladys could have caught sight of either of them outside the side door. She could have left the tea tray in the hall and gone out to see who it was and what they were doing. Whoever it was could have strangled her then and there and carried her body round to the clothesline and put the peg on her nose—"

"A crazy thing to do in all conscience! A nasty one, too."

"Yes, sir. That's what upset the old lady—Miss Marple, I mean. Nice old lady—and very shrewd. She's moved into the house to be near old Miss Ramsbottom, and I've no doubt she'll get to hear anything that's going."

"What's your next move, Neele?"

"I've an appointment with the London solicitors. I want to find out a little more about Rex Fortescue's affairs. And though it's old history, I want to hear a little more about the Blackbird Mine."

iii.

Mr. Billingsley, of Billingsley, Horsethorpe & Walters, was an urbane man whose discretion was concealed habitually by a misleadingly forthcoming manner. It was the second interview that Inspector Neele had had with him, and on this occasion. Mr. Billingsley's discretion was less noticeable than it had been on the former one. The triple tragedy at Yewtree Lodge had shaken Mr. Billingsley out of his professional reserve. He was now only too anxious to put all the facts he could before the police.

"Most extraordinary business, this whole thing," he

said. "A most extraordinary business. I don't remember anything like it in all my professional career."

"Frankly, Mr. Billingsley," said Inspector Neele, "we need all the help we can get."

"You can count on me, my dear sir. I shall be only too happy to assist you in every way I can."

"First let me ask you how well you knew the late Mr. Fortescue, and how well do you know the affairs of his firm?"

"I knew Rex Fortescue fairly well. That is to say I've known him for a period of, well, sixteen years, I should say. Mind you, we are not the only firm of solicitors he employed, not by a long way."

Inspector Neele nodded. He knew that. Billingsley, Horsethorpe & Walters were what one might describe as Rex Fortescue's reputable solicitors. For his less reputable dealings he had employed several different and slightly less scrupulous firms.

"Now what do you want to know?" continued Mr. Billingsley. "I've told you about his will. Percival Fortescue is the residuary legatee."

"I'm interested now," said Inspector Neele, "in the will of his widow. On Mr. Fortescue's death she came into the sum of one hundred thousand pounds, I understand?"

Billingsley nodded his head.

"A considerable sum of money," he said, "and I may tell you in confidence, Inspector, that it is one the firm could ill have afforded to pay out."

"The firm, then, is not prosperous?"

"Frankly," said Mr. Billingsley, "and strictly between ourselves, it's drifting on the rocks and has been for the last year and a half."

"For any particular reason?"

"Why, yes, I should say the reason was Rex Fortescue himself. For the last year Rex Fortescue's been acting like a madman. Selling good stock here, buying speculative stuff there, talking big about it all the time in the most extraordinary way. Wouldn't listen to advice. Percival—the son, you know—he came here urging me to use my influence with his father. He'd tried, apparently, and been swept aside. Well, I did what I could, but Fortescue wouldn't listen to reason. Really, he seems to have been a changed man."

"But not, I gather, a depressed man," said Inspector Neele.

"No, no. Quite the contrary. Flamboyant, bombastic."

Inspector Neele nodded. An idea which had already taken form in his mind was strengthened. He thought he was beginning to understand some of the causes of friction between Percival and his father. Mr. Billingsley was continuing.

"But it's no good asking me about the wife's will. I didn't make any will for her."

"No. I know that," said Neele. "I'm merely verifying that she had something to leave. In short, a hundred thousand pounds."

Mr. Billingsley was shaking his head violently.

"No, no, my dear sir. You're wrong there."

"Do you mean the hundred thousand pounds was only left to her for her lifetime?"

"No—no—it was left to her outright. But there was a clause in the will governing that bequest. That is to say, Fortescue's wife did not inherit the sum unless she survived him for one month. That, I may say, is a clause fairly common nowadays. It has come into operation owing to the uncertainties of air travel. If two people are killed in an air accident, it becomes exceedingly difficult to say who was the survivor and a lot of curious problems arise."

Inspector Neele was staring at him.

"Then Adele Fortescue had not got a hundred thousand pounds to leave. What happened to that money?"

"It goes back into the firm. Or rather, I should say, it goes to the residuary legatee."

"And the residuary legatee is Mr. Percival Fortescue."

"That's right," said Billingsley, "it goes to Percival Fortescue. And with the state the firm's affairs are in," he added unguardedly, "I should say that he'll need it!"

iv.

"The things you policemen want to know," said Inspector Neele's doctor friend.

"Come on, Bob, spill it."

"Well, as we're alone together you can't quote me, fortunately! But I should say, you know, that your idea's dead right. General Paralysis of the Insane, by the sound of it all. The family suspected it and wanted to get him to see a doctor. He wouldn't. It acts just in the way you describe. Loss of judgment, megalomania, violent fits of irritation and anger, boastfulness, delusions of grandeur—of being a great financial genius. Anyone suffering from that would soon put a solvent firm on the rocks, unless he could be restrained, and that's not so easy to do, especially if the man himself has an idea of what you're after. Yes, I should say it was a bit of luck for your friends that he died."

"They're no friends of mine," said Neele. He repeated what he had once said before:

"They're all very unpleasant people. . . ."

Chapter Nineteen

In the drawing-room at Yewtree Lodge, the whole
Fortescue family was assembled. Percival Fortescue,
leaning against the mantelpiece, was addressing the
meeting.

"It's all very well," said Percival. "But the whole position is most unsatisfactory. The police come and go
and don't tell us anything. One supposes they're pursu-
ing some line of research. In the meantime, everything's
at a standstill. One can't make plans, one can't arrange things for the future."

"It's all so inconsiderate," said Jennifer. "And so
stupid."

"There still seems to be this ban against anyone
leaving the house," went on Percival. "Still, I think
among ourselves we might discuss future plans. What
about you, Elaine? I gather you're going to marry—
what's-his-name—Gerald Wright? Have you any idea
when?"

"As soon as possible," said Elaine.

Percival frowned.

"You mean, in about six months' time?"

"No, I don't. Why should we wait six months?"

"I think it would be more decent," said Percival.

"Rubbish," said Elaine. "A month. That's the longest we'll wait."

"Well, it's for you to say," said Percival. "And what are your plans when you are married, if you have any?"

"We're thinking of starting a school."

Percival shook his head.

"That's a very risky speculation in these times. What with the shortage of domestic labor, the difficulty of getting an adequate teaching staff—really, Elaine, it sounds all right. But I should think twice about it if I were you."

"We have thought. Gerald feels that the whole future of this country lies in right education."

"I am seeing Mr. Billingsley the day after tomorrow," said Percival. "We've got to go into various questions of finance. He was suggesting that you might like to make this money that's been left to you by Father into a trust for yourself and your children. It's a very sound thing to do nowadays."

"I don't want to do that," said Elaine. "We shall need the money to start up our school. There's a very suitable house we've heard of for sale. It's in Cornwall. Beautiful grounds and quite a good house. It would have to be built onto a good deal—several wings added."

"You mean—you mean you're going to take all your money out of the business? Really, Elaine, I don't think you're wise."

"Much wiser to take it out than leave it in, I should say," said Elaine. "Businesses are going phut all over the place. You said yourself, Val, before Father died, that things were getting into a pretty bad state."

"One says that sort of thing," said Percival vaguely, "but I must say, Elaine, to take out all your capital and sink it in the buying, equipping and running of a school is crazy. If it's not a success, look what happens? You're left without a penny."

"It will be a success," said Elaine doggedly.

"I'm with you." Lance, lying sprawled out in a chair, spoke up encouragingly. "Have a crack at it, Elaine. In my opinion it'll be a damned odd sort of school, but it's what you want to do—you and Gerald. If you lose your money you'll at any rate have had the satisfaction of doing what you wanted to do."

"Just what one might have expected you to say, Lance," said Percival acidly.

"I know, I know," said Lance. "I'm the spendthrift prodigal son. But I still think I've had more fun out of life than you have, Percy, old boy."

"It depends on what you call fun," said Percival acidly. "Which brings us to your own plans, Lance. I suppose you'll be off again back to Kenya—or Canada—or climbing Mount Everest or something fairly fantastic?"

"Now what makes you think that?" said Lance.

"Well, you've never had much use for a stay-at-home life in England, have you?"

"One changes as one gets older," said Lance. "One settles down. D'you know, Percy my boy, I'm quite looking forward to having a crack at being a sober business man."

"Do you mean . . . ?"

"I mean I'm coming into the firm with you, old boy." Lance grinned. "Oh, you're the senior partner, of course. You've got the lion's share. I'm only a very junior partner. But I have got a holding in it that gives me the right to be in on things, doesn't it?"

"Well—yes—of course, if you put it that way. But I

can assure you, my dear boy, you'll be very, very bored."

"I wonder now. I don't believe I shall be bored."

Percival frowned.

"You don't seriously mean, Lance, that you're coming into the business?"

"Having a finger in the pie? Yes, that's exactly what I am doing."

Percival shook his head.

"Things are in a very bad way, you know. You'll find that out. It's going to be about all we can do to pay out Elaine her share, if she insists on having it paid out."

"There you are, Elaine," said Lance. "You see how wise you were to insist on grabbing your money while it's there to grab."

"Really, Lance," Percival spoke angrily, "these jokes of yours are in very bad taste."

"I do think, Lance, you might be more careful what you say," said Jennifer.

Sitting a little way away near the window, Pat studied them one by one. If this was what Lance had meant by twisting Percival's tail, she could see that he was achieving his object. Percival's neat impassivity was quite ruffled. He snapped again, angrily:

"Are you serious, Lance?"

"Dead serious."

"It won't work, you know. You'll soon get fed up."

"Not me. Think what a lovely change it'll be for me. A city office, typists running and going. I shall have a blonde secretary like Miss Grosvenor—is it Grosvenor? I suppose you've snaffled her. But I shall get one just the same. 'Yes, Mr. Lancelot, no, Mr. Lancelot. Your tea, Mr. Lancelot.' "

"Oh, don't play the fool," snapped Percival.

"Why are you so angry, my dear brother? Don't you look forward to having me share your city cares?"

"You haven't the least conception of the mess everything's in."

"No. You'll have to put me wise to all that."

"First, you've got to understand that for the last six months—no, more, a year—Father's not been himself. He's done the most incredibly foolish things, financially. Sold out good stock, acquired various wildcat holdings. Sometimes he's really thrown away money hand over fist. Just, one might say, for the fun of spending it."

"In fact," said Lance, "it's just as well for the family that he had taxine in his tea."

"That's a very ugly way of putting it, but in essence you're quite right. It's about the only thing that saved us from bankruptcy. But we shall have to be extremely conservative and go very cautiously for a bit."

Lance shook his head.

"I don't agree with you. Caution never does anyone any good. You must take a few risks, strike out. You must go for something big."

"I don't agree," said Percy. "Caution and economy. Those are our watchwords."

"Not mine," said Lance.

"You're only the junior partner, remember," said Percival.

"All right, all right. But I've got a little say-so all the same."

Percival walked up and down the room agitatedly.

"It's no good, Lance. I'm fond of you and all that—"

"Are you?" Lance interpolated. Percival did not appear to hear him.

". . . But I really don't think we're going to pull together at all. Our outlooks are totally different."

"That may be an advantage," said Lance.

"The only sensible thing," said Percival, "is to dissolve the partnership."

"You're going to buy me out—is that the idea?"

"My dear boy, it's the only sensible thing to do, with our ideas so different."

"If you find it hard to pay Elaine out her legacy, how are you going to manage to pay me my share?"

"Well, I didn't mean in cash," said Percival. "We could—er—divide up the holdings."

"With you taking the gilt-edged and me taking the worst of the speculative off you, I suppose?"

"They seem to be what you prefer," said Percival.

Lance grinned suddenly.

"You're right in a way, Percy, old boy. But I can't indulge my own taste entirely. I've got Pat here to think of."

Both men looked towards her. Pat opened her mouth, then shut it again. Whatever game Lance was playing, it was best that she should not interfere. That Lance was driving at something special, she was quite sure, but she was still a little uncertain as to what his actual object was.

"Line 'em up, Percy," said Lance, laughing. "Bogus Diamond Mines, Inaccessible Rubies, the Oil Concessions where no oil is. Do you think I'm quite as big a fool as I look?"

Percival said:

"Of course, some of these holdings are highly speculative, but remember, they may turn out immensely valuable."

"Changed your tune, haven't you?" said Lance, grinning. "Going to offer me Father's latest wildcat acquisitions as well as the old Blackbird Mine and things of that kind. By the way, has the Inspector been asking you about this Blackbird Mine?"

Percival frowned.

"Yes, he did. I can't imagine what he wanted to know about it. I couldn't tell him much. You and I were children at the time. I just remember vaguely that Father went out there and came back saying the whole thing was no good."

"What was it—a gold mine?"

"I believe so. Father came back pretty certain that there was no gold there. And, mind you, he wasn't the sort of man to be mistaken."

"Who got him into it? A man called MacKenzie, wasn't it?"

"Yes. MacKenzie died out there."

"MacKenzie died out there," said Lance thoughtfully. "Wasn't there a terrific scene? I seem to remember. . . . Mrs. MacKenzie, wasn't it? Came here. Ranted and stormed at Father. Hurled down curses on his head. She accused him, if I remember rightly, of murdering her husband."

"Really," said Percival repressively. "I can't recollect anything of the kind."

"I remember it, though," said Lance. "I was a good bit younger than you, of course. Perhaps that's why it appealed to me. As a child it struck me as full of drama. Where was Blackbird? West Africa, wasn't it?"

"Yes, I think so."

"I must look up the concession sometime," said Lance, "when I'm at the office."

"You can be quite sure," said Percival, "that Father made no mistake. If he came back saying there was no gold, there was no gold."

"You're probably right there," said Lance. "Poor Mrs. MacKenzie. I wonder what happened to her and to those two kids she brought along. Funny—they must be grown up by now."

Chapter Twenty

At the Pinewood Private Sanatorium, Inspector Neele, sitting in the visitors' parlor, was facing a gray-haired, elderly lady. Helen MacKenzie was sixty-three, though she looked younger. She had pale blue, rather vacant-looking eyes, and a weak, indeterminate chin. She had a long upper lip which occasionally twitched. She held a large book in her lap and was looking down at it as Inspector Neele talked to her. In Inspector Neele's mind was the conversation he had just had with Doctor Crosbie, the head of the establishment.

"She's a voluntary patient, of course," said Doctor Crosbie, "not certified."

"She's not dangerous, then?"

"Oh, no. Most of the time she's as sane to talk to as you or I. It's one of her good periods now so that you'll be able to have a perfectly normal conversation with her."

Bearing this in mind, Inspector Neele started his first conversation essay.

"It's very kind of you to see me, madam," he said. "My name is Neele. I've come to see you about a Mr. Fortescue who has recently died. A Mr. Fortescue. I expect you know the name."

Mrs. MacKenzie's eyes were fixed on her book. She said:

"I don't know what you're talking about."

"Mr. Fortescue, madam. Mr. Rex Fortescue."

"No," said Mrs. MacKenzie. "No. Certainly not."

Inspector Neele was slightly taken aback. He wondered whether this was what Doctor Crosbie called being completely normal.

"I think, Mrs. MacKenzie, you knew him a good many years ago."

"Not really," said Mrs. MacKenzie. "It was yesterday."

"I see," said Inspector Neele, falling back upon his formula rather uncertainly. "I believe," he went on, "that you paid him a visit many years ago at his residence, Yewtree Lodge."

"A very ostentatious house," said Mrs. MacKenzie.

"Yes. Yes, you might call it that. He had been connected with your husband, I believe, over a certain mine in Africa. The Blackbird Mine, I believe, it was called."

"I have to read my book," said Mrs. MacKenzie. "There's not much time and I have to read my book."

"Yes, madam. Yes, I quite see that." There was a pause, then Inspector Neele went on, "Mr. MacKenzie and Mr. Fortescue went out together to Africa to survey the mine."

"It was my husband's mine," said Mrs. MacKenzie. "He found it and staked a claim to it. He wanted money to capitalize it. He went to Rex Fortescue. If

I'd been wiser, if I'd known more, I wouldn't have let him do it."

"No, I see that. As it was, they went out together to Africa, and there your husband died of fever."

"I must read my book," said Mrs. MacKenzie.

"Do you think Mr. Fortescue swindled your husband over the Blackbird Mine, Mrs. MacKenzie?"

Without raising her eyes from the book, Mrs. Mac-Kenzie said, "How stupid you are."

"Yes, yes, I dare say. . . . But you see, it's all a long time ago and making inquiries about a thing that is over a long time ago is rather difficult."

"Who said it was over?"

"I see. You don't think it is over?"

" 'No question is ever settled until it is settled right.' Kipling said that. Nobody reads Kipling nowadays, but he was a great man."

"Do you think the question will be settled right one of these days?"

"Rex Fortescue is dead, isn't he? You said so."

"He was poisoned," said Inspector Neele.

Rather disconcertingly, Mrs. MacKenzie laughed.

"What nonsense," she said, "he died of fever."

"I'm talking about Mr. Rex Fortescue."

"So am I. "She looked up suddenly and her pale blue eyes fixed his. "Come now," she said, "he died in his bed, didn't he? He died in his bed?"

"He died in St. Jude's Hospital," said Inspector Neele.

"Nobody knows where my husband died," said Mrs. MacKenzie. "Nobody knows how he died or where he was buried. . . . All anyone knows is what Rex Fortescue said. And Rex Fortescue was a liar!"

"Do you think there may have been foul play?"

"Foul play, foul play, fowls lay eggs, don't they?"

"You think that Rex Fortescue was responsible for your husband's death?"

"I had an egg for breakfast this morning," said Mrs. MacKenzie. "Quite fresh, too. Surprising, isn't it, when one thinks that it was thirty years ago?"

Neele drew a deep breath. It seemed unlikely that he was ever going to get anywhere at this rate, but he persevered. "Somebody put dead blackbirds on Rex Fortescue's desk about a month or two before he died."

"That's interesting. That's very, very interesting."

"Have you any idea, madam, who might have done that?"

"Ideas aren't any help to one. One has to have action. I brought them up for that, you know, to take action."

"You're talking about your children?"

She nodded her head rapidly.

"Yes. Donald and Ruby. They were nine and seven and left without a father. I told them. I told them every day. I made them swear it every night."

Inspector Neele leant forward.

"What did you make them swear?"

"That they'd kill him, of course."

"I see."

Inspector Neele spoke as though it was the most reasonable remark in the world.

"Did they?"

"Donald went to Dunkirk. He never came back. They sent me a wire saying he was dead. 'Deeply regret killed in action.' Action, you see, the wrong kind of action."

"I'm sorry to hear that, madam. What about your daughter?"

"I haven't got a daughter," said Mrs. Mackenzie.

"You spoke of her just now," said Neele. "Your daughter Ruby."

"Ruby. Yes, Ruby." She leaned forward. "Do you know what I've done to Ruby?"

"No, madam. What have you done to her?"

She whispered suddenly,

"Look here at the Book."

He saw then that what she was holding in her lap was a Bible. It was a very old Bible and as she opened it, on the front page, Inspector Neele saw various names had been written. It was obviously a family Bible in which the old-fashioned custom had been continued of entering each new birth. Mrs. MacKenzie's thin finger pointed to the two last names. "Donald MacKenzie" with the date of his birth, and "Ruby MacKenzie" with the date of hers. But a thick line was drawn through Ruby MacKenzie's name.

"You see?" said Mrs. MacKenzie. "I struck her out of the Book. I cut her off forever! The Recording Angel won't find her name there."

"You cut her name out of the Book? Now, why, madam?"

Mrs. MacKenzie looked at him cunningly.

"You know why," she said.

"But I don't. Really, madam, I don't."

"She didn't keep faith. You know she didn't keep faith."

"Where is your daughter now, madam?"

"I've told you. I have no daughter. There isn't such a person as Ruby MacKenzie any longer."

"You mean she's dead?"

"Dead?" The woman laughed suddenly. "It would be much better for her if she were dead. Much better. Much, much better." She sighed and turned restlessly in her seat. Then, her manner reverting to a kind of formal courtesy, she said, " "I'm so sorry, but really I'm afraid I can't talk to you any longer. You see, the time is getting very short, and I must read my book."

To Inspector Neele's further remarks Mrs. Mac-Kenzie returned no reply. She merely made a faint gesture of annoyance and continued to read her Bible with her finger following the line of the verse she was reading.

Neele got up and left. He had another brief interview with the Superintendent.

"Do any of her relations come to see her?" he asked. "A daughter, for instance?"

"I believe a daughter did come to see her in my predecessor's time, but her visit agitated the patient so much that he advised her not to come again. Since then everything is arranged through solicitors."

"And you've no idea where this Ruby MacKenzie is now?"

The Superintendent shook his head.

"No idea whatsoever."

"You've no idea whether she's married, for instance?"

"I don't know. All I can do is to give you the address of the solicitors who deal with us."

Inspector Neele had already tracked down those solicitors. They were unable, or said they were unable, to tell him anything. A trust fund had been established for Mrs. MacKenzie, which they managed. These arrangements had been made some years previously, and they had not seen Miss MacKenzie since.

Inspector Neele tried to get a description of Ruby MacKenzie, but the results were not encouraging. So many relations came to visit patients that after a lapse of years they were bound to be remembered dimly, with the appearance of one mixed up with the appearance of another. The Matron, who had been there for many years, seemed to remember that Miss MacKenzie was small and dark. The only other nurse who had been there for any length of time recalled that she was heavily built and fair.

"So there we are, sir," said Inspector Neele as he reported to the Assistant Commissioner. "There's a whole crazy setup and it fits together. It must mean something."

The A.C. nodded thoughtfully.

"The blackbirds in the pie tying up with the Blackbird Mine, rye in the dead man's pocket, bread and honey with Adele Fortescue's tea (not that that is conclusive. After all, anyone might have had bread and honey for tea!). The third murder, that girl strangled with a stocking and a clothes peg nipped onto her nose. Yes, crazy as the setup is, it certainly can't be ignored."

"Half a minute, sir," said Inspector Neele.

"What is it?"

Neele was frowning.

"You know, what you've just said. It didn't ring true. It was wrong somewhere." He shook his head and sighed. "No. I can't place it."

Chapter Twenty-one

Lance and Pat wandered round the well-kept grounds surrounding Yewtree Lodge.

"I hope I'm not hurting your feelings, Lance," Pat murmured, "if I say this is quite the nastiest garden I've been in."

"It won't hurt my feelings," said Lance. "Is it? Really I don't know. It seems to have three gardeners working on it very industriously."

Pat said, "Probably that's what's wrong with it. No expense spared, no signs of individual taste. All the right rhododendrons and all the right bedding out, done in the proper season, I expect."

"Well, what would you put in an English garden, Pat, if you had one?"

"My garden," said Pat, "would have hollyhocks, larkspurs and Canterbury bells, no bedding out and none of these horrible yews."

She glanced up at the dark yew hedges disparagingly.

"Association of ideas," said Lance easily.

"There's something awfully frightening about a poisoner," said Pat. "I mean, it must be a horrid, brooding, revengeful mind."

"So that's how you see it? Funny! I just think of it as businesslike and cold-blooded."

"I suppose one could look at it that way." She resumed, with a slight shiver, "All the same, to do three murders. . . . Whoever did it must be mad."

"Yes," said Lance, in a low voice. "I'm afraid so." Then, breaking out sharply, he said, "For God's sake, Pat, do go away from here. Go back to London. Go down to Devonshire or up to the Lakes. Go to Stratford on Avon or go and look at the Norfolk Broads. The police wouldn't mind your going—you had nothing to do with this. You were in Paris when the old man was killed and in London when the other two died. I tell you it worries me to death to have you here."

Pat paused a moment before saying quietly:

"You know who it is, don't you?"

"No, I don't."

"But you think you know. . . . That's why you're frightened for me. I wish you'd tell me."

"I can't tell you. I don't know anything. But I wish to God you'd go away from here."

"Darling," said Pat, "I'm not going. I'm staying here. For better, for worse. That's how I feel about it." She added, with a sudden catch in her voice, "Only with me it's always for worse."

"What on earth do you mean, Pat?"

"I bring bad luck. That's what I mean. I bring bad luck to anybody I come in contact with."

"My dear, adorable nitwit, you haven't brought bad luck to me. Look how after I married you the old man sent for me to come home and make friends with him."

"Yes, and what happened when you did come home? I tell you, I'm unlucky to people."

"Look here, my sweet, you've got a thing about all this. It's superstition, pure and simple."

"I can't help it. Some people do bring bad luck. I'm one of them."

Lance took her by the shoulders and shook her violently. "You're my Pat and to be married to you is the greatest luck in the world. So get that into your silly head." Then, calming down, he said in a more sober voice, "But seriously, Pat, do be very careful. If there is someone unhinged round here, I don't want you to be the one who stops the bullet or drinks the henbane."

"Or drinks the henbane, as you say."

"When I'm not around, stick to that old lady. What's-her-name Marple. Why do you think Aunt Effie asked her to stay here?"

"Goodness knows why Aunt Effie does anything. Lance, how long are we going to stay here?"

Lance shrugged his shoulders.

"Difficult to say."

"I don't think," said Pat, "that we're really awfully welcome." She hesitated as she spoke the words. "The house belongs to your brother now, I suppose? He doesn't really want us here, does he?"

Lance chuckled suddenly.

"Not he, but he's got to stick us for the present, at any rate."

"And afterwards? What are we going to do, Lance? Are we going back to East Africa, or what?"

"Is that what you'd like to do, Pat?"

She nodded vigorously.

"That's lucky," said Lance, "because it's what I'd like to do, too. I don't take much to this country nowadays."

Pat's face brightened.

"How lovely. From what you said the other day, I was afraid you might want to stop here."

A devilish glint appeared in Lance's eyes.

"You're to hold your tongue about our plans, Pat," he said. "I have it in my mind to twist dear brother Percival's tail a bit."

"Oh, Lance, do be careful."

"I'll be careful, my sweet, but I don't see why old Percy should get away with everything."

ii.

With her head a little on one side, looking like an amiable cockatoo, Miss Marple sat in the large drawing-room listening to Mrs. Percival Fortescue. Miss Marple looked particularly incongruous in the drawing-room. Her light, spare figure was alien to the vast, brocaded sofa in which she sat, with its many-hued cushions strewn around her. Miss Marple sat very upright because she had been taught to use a back-board as a girl, and not to loll. In a large armchair beside her, dressed in elaborate black, was Mrs. Percival, talking away volubly at nineteen to the dozen. "Exactly," thought Miss Marple, "like poor Mrs. Emmett, the bank manager's wife." She remembered how one day Mrs. Emmett had come to call and talk about the selling arrangements for Poppy Day, and how after the preliminary business had been settled, Mrs. Emmett had suddenly begun to talk and talk and talk. Mrs. Emmett occupied rather a difficult position in St. Mary Meade. She did not belong to the old guard of ladies in reduced circumstances who lived in neat houses round the church, and who knew intimately all the ramifications of the County families, even though they might not be strictly county themselves. Mr. Emmett, the bank manager, had undeniably married beneath him and the

result was that his wife was in a position of great loneliness since she could not, of course, associate with the
wives of trades people. Snobbery here raised its hideous
head and marooned Mrs. Emmett on a permanent
island of loneliness.

The necessity to talk grew upon Mrs. Emmett, and
on that particular day it had burst its bounds, and Miss
Marple had received the full flood of the torrent. She
had been sorry for Mrs. Emmett then, and today she
was rather sorry for Mrs. Percival Fortescue.

Mrs. Percival had had a lot of grievances to bear and
the relief of airing them to a more or less total stranger
was enormous.

"Of course, I never want to complain," said Mrs.
Percival. "I've never been of the complaining kind.
What I always say is that one must put up with things.
What can't be cured must be endured and I'm sure
I've never said a word to anyone. It's really difficult
to know whom I could have spoken to. In some ways
one is very isolated here—very isolated. It's very convenient, of course, and a great saving of expense to have
our own set of rooms in this house. But, of course, it's
not at all like having a place of your own. I'm sure you
agree."

Miss Marple said she agreed.

"Fortunately, our new house is almost ready to move
into. It is a question really of getting the painters and
decorators out. These men are so slow. My husband, of
course, has been quite satisfied living here. But then
it's different for a man. That's what I always say—it's so
different for a man. Don't you agree?"

Miss Marple agreed that it was very different for a
man. She could say this without a qualm as it was what
she really believed. "The gentlemen" were, in Miss
Marple's mind, in a totally different category from her
own sex. They required two eggs plus bacon for break-

fast, three good nourishing meals a day, and were never to be contradicted or argued with before dinner. Mrs. Percival went on:

"My husband, you see, is away all day in the city. When he comes home he's just tired and wants to sit down and read. But I, on the contrary, am alone here all day with no congenial company at all. I've been perfectly comfortable and all that. Excellent food. But what I do feel one needs is a really pleasant social circle. The people round here are really not my kind. Part of them are what I call a flashy, bridge-playing lot. Not nice bridge. I like a hand of bridge myself as well as anybody, but of course they're all very rich down here. They play for enormously high stakes, and there's a great deal of drinking. In fact, the sort of life that I call really fast society. Then, of course, there's a sprinkling of—well, you can only call them old pussies who love to potter round with a trowel and do gardening."

Miss Marple looked slightly guilty, since she was herself an inveterate gardener.

"I don't want to say anything against the dead," resumed Mrs. Percy rapidly, "but there's no doubt about it, Mr. Fortescue, my father-in-law, I mean, made a very foolish second marriage. My—well, I can't call her my mother-in-law, she was the same age as I am. The real truth of it is she was man-mad. Absolutely man-mad. And the way she spent money! My father-in-law was an absolute fool about her. Didn't care what bills she ran up. It vexed Percy very much, very much indeed. Percy is always so careful about money matters. He hates waste. And then what with Mr. Fortescue being so peculiar and so bad-tempered, flashing out in these terrible rages, spending money like water, backing wildcat schemes. Well—it wasn't at all nice."

Miss Marple ventured upon making a remark.

"That must have worried your husband, too?"

"Oh yes, it did. For the last year Percy's been very worried, indeed. It's really made him quite different. His manner, you know, changed even towards me. Sometimes when I talked to him he used not to answer." Mrs. Percy sighed, then went on, "Then Elaine, my sister-in-law, you know, she's a very odd sort of girl. Very out-of-doors and all that. Not exactly unfriendly but not sympathetic, you know. She never wanted to go up to London to shop, or go to a matinée or anything of that kind. She wasn't even interested in clothes." Mrs. Percival sighed again and murmured, "But, of course, I don't want to complain in any way." A qualm of compunction came over her. She said, hurriedly: "You must think it most odd, talking to you like this when you are a comparative stranger. But really, what with all the strain and shock—I think really it's the shock that matters most. Delayed shock. I feel so nervous, you know, that I really—well, I really must speak to someone. You remind me so much of a dear old lady, Miss Trefusis James. She fractured her femur when she was seventy-five. It was a very long business nursing her, and we became great friends. She gave me a fox fur cape when I left and I did think it was kind of her."

"I know just how you feel," said Miss Marple.

And this again was true. Mrs. Percival's husband was obviously bored by her and paid very little attention to her, and the poor woman had managed to make no local friends. Running up to London and shopping, matinées and a luxurious house to live in did not make up for the lack of humanity in her relations with her husband's family.

"I hope it's not rude of me to say so," said Miss Marple in a gentle, old lady's voice, "but I really feel that the late Mr. Fortescue cannot have been a very nice man."

"He wasn't," said his daughter-in-law. "Quite frankly, my dear, between you and me, he was a detestable old man. I don't wonder—I really don't—that someone put him out of the way."

"You've no idea at all who—" began Miss Marple and broke off. "Oh dear, perhaps this is a question I should not ask—not even an idea who—who—well, who it might have been?"

"Oh, I think it was that horrible man, Crump," said Mrs. Percival. "I've always disliked him very much. He's got a manner, not really rude, you know, but yet it is rude. Impertinent, that's more it."

"Still, there would have to be a motive, I suppose."

"I really don't know that that sort of person requires much motive. I daresay Mr. Fortescue ticked him off about something, and I rather suspect that sometimes he drinks too much. But what I really think is that he's a bit unbalanced, you know. Like that footman, or butler, whoever it was, who went round the house shooting everybody. Of course, to be quite honest with you, I did suspect that it was Adele who poisoned Mr. Fortescue. But now, of course, one can't suspect that since she's been poisoned herself. She may have accused Crump, you know. And then he lost his head and perhaps managed to put something in the sandwiches and Gladys saw him do it and so he killed her too. I think it's really dangerous having him in the house at all. Oh dear, I wish I could get away, but I suppose these horrible policemen won't let one do anything of the kind." She leant forward impulsively and put a plump hand on Miss Marple's arm. "Sometimes I feel I must get away —that if it doesn't all stop soon I shall—I shall actually run away—"

She leant back studying Miss Marple's face.

"But perhaps—that wouldn't be wise?"

"No, I don't think it would be very wise. The police could soon find you, you know."

"Could they? Could they really? You think they're clever enough for that?"

"It is very foolish to underestimate the police. Inspector Neele strikes me as a particularly intelligent man."

"Oh! I thought he was rather stupid."

Miss Marple shook her head.

"I can't help feeling—" Jennifer Fortescue hesitated —"that it's dangerous to stay here."

"Dangerous for you, you mean?"

"Ye-es—well, yes—"

"Because of something you—know?"

Mrs. Percival seemed to take breath.

"Oh no, of course. I don't know anything. What should I know? It's just—just that I'm nervous. That man Crump—"

But it was not, Miss Marple thought, of Crump that Mrs. Percival Fortescue was thinking, watching the clenching and unclenching of Jennifer's hands. Miss Marple thought that for some reason Jennifer Fortescue was very badly frightened indeed.

Chapter Twenty-two

It was growing dark. Miss Marple had taken her knitting over to the window in the library. Looking out of the glass pane, she saw Pat Fortescue walking up and down the terrace outside. Miss Marple unlatched the window and called through it.

"Come in, my dear. Do come in. I'm sure it's much too cold and damp for you to be out there without a coat on."

Pat obeyed the summons. She came in and shut the window and turned on two of the lamps.

"Yes," she said, "it's not a very nice afternoon." She sat down on the sofa by Miss Marple. "What are you knitting?"

"Oh, just a little matinée coat, dear. For a baby, you know. I always say young mothers can't have too many matinée coats for their babies. It's the second size. I always knit the second size. Babies so soon grow out of the first size."

Pat stretched out long legs towards the fire.

"It's nice in here today," she said "With the fire and the lamps and you knitting things for babies. It all seems cozy and homely and as England ought to be."

"It's as England is," said Miss Marple. "There are not so many Yewtree Lodges, my dear."

"I think that's a good thing," said Pat. "I don't believe this was ever a happy house. I don't believe anybody was ever happy in it, in spite of all the money they spent and the things they had."

"No," Miss Marple agreed. "I shouldn't say it had been a happy house."

"I suppose Adele may have been happy," said Pat. "I never met her, of course, so I don't know, but Jennifer is pretty miserable and Elaine's been eating her heart out over a young man who she probably knows in her heart of hearts doesn't care for her. Oh, how I want to get away from here!" She looked at Miss Marple and smiled suddenly. "D'you know," she said, "that Lance told me to stick as close to you as I could? He seemed to think I should be safe that way."

"Your husband's no fool," said Miss Marple.

"No. Lance isn't a fool. At least, he is in some ways. But I wish he'd tell me exactly what he's afraid of. One thing seems clear enough. Somebody in this house is mad, and madness is always frightening because you don't know how mad people's minds will work. You don't know what they'll do next."

"My poor child," said Miss Marple.

"Oh, I'm all right, really. I ought to be tough enough by now."

Miss Marple said gently, "You've had a good deal of unhappiness, haven't you, my dear?"

"Oh, I've had some very good times, too. I had a lovely childhood in Ireland, riding, hunting, and a great big, bare draughty house with lots and lots of sun in it.

If you've had a happy childhood, nobody can take that away from you, can they? It was afterwards—when I grew up—that things seemed always to go wrong. To begin with, I suppose, it was the war."

"Your husband was a fighter pilot, wasn't he?"

"Yes. We'd only been married a month when Don was shot down." She stared ahead of her into the fire. "I thought at first I wanted to die, too. It seemed so unfair, so cruel. And yet—in the end—I almost began to see that it had been the best thing. Don was wonderful in the war. Brave and reckless and gay. He had all the qualities that are needed, wanted in a war. But I don't believe, somehow, peace would have suited him. He had a kind of—oh, how shall I put it?—arrogant insubordination. He wouldn't have fitted in or settled down. He'd have fought against things. He was, well, antisocial in a way. No, he wouldn't have fitted in."

"It's wise of you to see that, my dear." Miss Marple bent over her knitting, picked up a stitch, counted under her breath, "Three plain, two purl, slip one, knit two together," and then said, aloud, "And your second husband, my dear?"

"Freddy? Freddy shot himself."

"Oh dear. How very sad. What a tragedy."

"We were very happy together," said Pat. "I began to realize, about two years ago after we were married, that Freddy wasn't—well, wasn't always straight. I began to find out the sort of things that were going on. But it didn't seem to matter, between us two, that is. Because, you see, Freddy loved me and I loved him. I tried not to know what was going on. That was cowardly of me, I suppose, but I couldn't have changed him, you know. You can't change people."

"No," said Miss Marple, "you can't change people."

"I'd taken him and loved him and married him for what he was, and I sort of felt that I just had to—put up with it. Then things went wrong and he couldn't face it, and he shot himself. After he died I went out to Kenya to stay with some friends there. I couldn't stop on in England and go on meeting all—all the old crowd that knew about it all. And out in Kenya I met Lance." Her face changed and softened. She went on looking into the fire, and Miss Marple looked at her. Presently Pat turned her head and said, "Tell me, Miss Marple, what do you really think of Percival?"

"Well, I've not seen very much of him. Just at breakfast, usually. That's all. I don't think he very much likes my being here."

Pat laughed suddenly.

"He's mean, you know. Terribly mean about money. Lance says he always was. Jennifer complains of it, too. Goes over the housekeeping accounts with Miss Dove. Complaining of every item. But Miss Dove manages to hold her own. She's rather a wonderful person. Don't you think so?"

"Yes, indeed. She reminds me of Mrs. Latimer in my own village, St. Mary Meade. She ran the Women's Voluntary Services, you know, and the Girl Guides, and indeed, she ran practically everything there. It wasn't for quite five years that we discovered that—oh, but I mustn't gossip. Nothing is more boring than people talking to you about places and people whom you've never seen and know nothing about. You must forgive me, my dear."

"Is St. Mary Meade a very nice village?"

"Well, I don't quite know what you would call a nice village, my dear. It's quite a pretty village. There are some nice people living in it and some extremely unpleasant people as well. Very curious things go on there just as in any other village. Human nature is much the same everywhere, is it not?"

"You go up and see Miss Ramsbottom a good deal, don't you?" said Pat. "Now, she really frightens me."

"Frightens you? Why?"

"Because I think she's crazy. I think she's got religious mania. You don't think she could be—really—mad, do you?"

"In what way mad?"

"Oh, you know what I mean, Miss Marple, well enough. She sits up there and never goes out, and broods about sin. Well, she might have felt in the end that it was her mission in life to execute judgment."

"Is that what your husband thinks?"

"I don't know what Lance thinks. He won't tell me. But I'm quite sure of one thing—that he believes that it's someone who's mad, and it's someone in the family. Well, Percival's sane enough, I should say. Jennifer's just stupid and rather pathetic. She's a bit nervy, but that's all, and Elaine is one of those queer, tempestuous, tense girls. She's desperately in love with this young man of hers and she'll never admit to herself for a moment that he's marrying her for her money."

"You think he is marrying her for money?"

"Yes, I do. Don't you think so?"

"I should say so quite certainly," said Miss Marple. "Like young Ellis who married Marion Bates, the rich ironmonger's daughter. She was a very plain girl and absolutely besotted about him. However, it turned out quite well. People like young Ellis and this Gerald Wright are only really disagreeable when they've married a poor girl for love. They are so annoyed with themselves for doing it that they take it out on the girl. But if they marry a rich girl they continue to respect her."

"I don't see," went on Pat, frowning, "how it can be anyone from outside. And so—and so that accounts for the atmosphere that is here. Everyone watching everybody else. Only something's got to happen soon—"

"There won't be any more deaths," said Miss Marple. "At least, I shouldn't think so."

"You can't be sure of that."

"Well, as a matter of fact, I am fairly sure. The murderer's accomplished his purpose, you see."

"His?"

"Well, his or her. One says his for convenience."

"You say his or her purpose. What sort of purpose?"

Miss Marple shook her head—she was not yet quite sure herself.

Chapter Twenty-three

Once again Miss Somers had just made tea in the typists' room, and once again the kettle had not been boiling when Miss Somers poured the water onto the tea. History repeats itself. Miss Griffith, accepting her cup, thought to herself, I really must speak to Mr. Percival about Somers. I'm sure we can do better. But with all this terrible business going on, one doesn't like to bother him over office details.

As so often before, Miss Griffith said sharply, "Water not boiling again, Somers."

Miss Somers, going pink, replied in her usual formula, "Oh, dear, I was sure it was boiling this time."

Further developments on the same line were interrupted by the entrance of Lance Fortescue. He looked round him somewhat vaguely, and Miss Griffith, jumping up, came forward to meet him.

"Mr. Lance!" she exclaimed.

He swung round towards her and his face lit up in a smile.

"Hullo. Why, it's Miss Griffith."

Miss Griffith was delighted. Eleven years since he had seen her and he knew her name. She said in a confused voice, "Fancy your remembering."

And Lance said easily, with all his charm to the fore, "Of course I remember."

A flicker of excitement was running round the typists' room. Miss Somers' troubles over the tea were forgotten. She was gaping at Lance with her mouth slightly open. Miss Bell gazed eagerly over the top of her typewriter and Miss Chase unobtrusively drew out her compact and powdered her nose. Lance Fortescue looked round him.

"So everything's still going on just the same here," he said.

"Not many changes, Mr. Lance. How brown you look and how well! I suppose you must have had a very interesting life abroad."

"You could call it that," said Lance, "but perhaps I am now going to try and have an interesting life in London."

"You're coming back here to the office?"

"Maybe."

"Oh, but how delightful."

"You'll find me very rusty," said Lance. "You'll have to show me all the ropes, Miss Griffith."

Miss Griffith laughed delightedly.

"It will be very nice to have you back, Mr. Lance. Very nice indeed."

Lance threw her an appreciative glance.

"That's sweet of you," he said. "That's very sweet of you."

"We never believed—none of us thought . . ." Miss Griffith broke off and flushed.

Lance patted her on the arm.

"You didn't believe the devil was as black as he was painted? Well, perhaps he wasn't. But that's all old history now. There's no good going back over it. The future's the thing." He added, "Is my brother here?"

"He's in the inner office, I think."

Lance nodded easily and passed on. In the ante-room to the inner sanctum a hard-faced woman of middle age rose behind a desk and said forbiddingly, "Your name and business, please?"

Lance looked at her doubtfully.

"Are you—Miss Grosvenor?" he asked.

Miss Grosvenor had been described to him as a glamorous blonde. She had, indeed, appeared so in the pictures that had been published in the newspapers reporting the inquest on Rex Fortescue. This, surely, could not be Miss Grosvenor.

"Miss Grosvenor left last week. I am Mrs. Hardcastle, Mr. Percival Fortescue's personal secretary."

How like old Percy, thought Lance. To get rid of a glamorous blonde and take on a Gorgon instead. I wonder why? Was it safety or was it because this one comes cheaper? Aloud he said easily, "I'm Lancelot Fortescue. You haven't met me yet."

"Oh, I'm sorry, Mr. Lancelot," Mrs. Hardcastle apologized. "This is the first time, I think, you've been to the office?"

"The first time but not the last," said Lance, smiling.

He crossed the room and opened the door of what had been his father's private office. Somewhat to his surprise, it was not Percival who was sitting behind the desk there, but Inspector Neele. Inspector Neele looked up from a large wad of papers which he was sorting, and nodded his head.

"Good morning, Mr. Fortescue, you've come to take up your duties, I suppose."

"So you've heard I decided to come into the firm?"

"Your brother told me so."

"He did, did he? With enthusiasm?"

Inspector Neele endeavored to conceal a smile.

"The enthusiasm was not marked," he said gravely.

"Poor Percy," commented Lance.

Inspector Neele looked at him curiously.

"Are you really going to become a City man?"

"You don't think it's likely, Inspector Neele?"

"It doesn't seem quite in character, Mr. Fortescue."

"Why not? I'm my father's son."

"And your mother's."

Lance shook his head.

"You haven't got anything there, Inspector. My mother was a Victorian romantic. Her favorite reading was the *Idylls of the King,* as indeed you may have deduced from our curious Christian names. She was an invalid and always, I should imagine, out of touch with reality. I'm not like that at all. I have no sentiment, very little sense of romance, and I'm a realist first and last."

"People aren't always what they think themselves to be," Inspector Neele pointed out.

"No, I suppose that's true," said Lance.

He sat down in a chair and stretched his long legs out in his own characteristic fashion. He was smiling to himself. Then he said unexpectedly, "You're shrewder than my brother, Inspector."

"In what way, Mr. Fortescue?"

"I've put the wind up Percy, all right. He thinks he's going to have my fingers fiddling about in his pie. He thinks I'll launch out and spend the firm's money and try and embroil him in wildcat schemes. It would be almost worth doing just for the fun of it! Almost, but not quite. I couldn't really stand an office life, Inspector. I like the open air and some possibilities of adventure. I'd stifle in a place like this." He added quickly, "This is off the record, mind. Don't give me away to Percy, will you?"

"I don't suppose the subject will arise, Mr. Fortescue."

"I must have my bit of fun with Percy," said Lance. "I want to make him sweat a bit. I've got to get a bit of my own back."

"That's rather a curious phrase, Mr. Fortescue," said Neele. "Your own back—for what?"

Lance shrugged his shoulders.

"Oh, it's old history now. Not worth going back over."

"There was a little matter of a check, I understand, in the past. Would that be what you're referring to?"

"How much you know, Inspector!"

"There was no question of prosecution, I understand," said Neele. "Your father wouldn't have done that."

"No. He just kicked me out, that's all."

Inspector Neele eyed him speculatively, but it was not Lance Fortescue of whom he was thinking, but of Percival. The honest, industrious, parsimonious Percival. It seemed to him that wherever he got in the case he was always coming up against the enigma of Percival Fortescue, a man of whom everybody knew the outer aspects, but whose inner personality was much harder to gauge. One would have said from observing him, a somewhat colorless and insignificant character, a man who had been very much under his father's thumb. Percy Prim, in fact, as the A.C. had once said. Neele was trying now, through Lance, to get a closer appreciation of Percival's personality. He murmured in a tentative manner:

"Your brother seems always to have been very much —well, how shall I put it—under your father's thumb."

"I wonder." Lance seemed definitely to be considering the point. "I wonder. Yes, that would be the effect,

I think, given. But I'm not sure that it was really the truth. It's astonishing, you know, when I look back through life, to see how Percy always got his own way without seeming to do so, if you know what I mean."

Yes, Inspector Neele thought, it was indeed astonishing. He sorted through the papers in front of him, fished out a letter and shoved it across the desk towards Lance.

"This is a letter you wrote last August, isn't it, Mr. Fortescue?"

Lance took it, glanced at it and returned it.

"Yes," he said, "I wrote it after I got back to Kenya last summer. Dad kept it, did he? Where was it—here in the office?"

"No, Mr. Fortescue, it was among your father's papers in Yewtree Lodge."

The Inspector considered it speculatively as it lay on the desk in front of him. It was not a long letter.

"Dear Dad, I've talked things over with Pat and I agree to your proposition. It will take me a little time to get things fixed up here, say about the end of October or beginning of November. I'll let you know nearer the time. I hope we'll pull together better than we used to do. Anyway, I'll do my best. I can't say more. Look after yourself. Yours, Lance."

"Where did you address this letter, Mr. Fortescue? To the office or Yewtree Lodge?"

Lance frowned in an effort of recollection.

"It's difficult. I can't remember. You see, it's almost three months now. The office, I think. Yes, I'm almost sure. Here to the office." He paused a moment before asking with frank curiosity, "Why?"

"I wondered," said Inspector Neele. "Your father did not put it in the file here among his private papers. He took it back with him to Yewtree Lodge, and I found it in his desk there. I wondered why he should have done that."

Lance laughed.

"To keep it out of Percy's way, I suppose."

"Yes," said Inspector Neele, "it would seem so. Your brother, then, had access to your father's private papers here?"

"Well," Lance hesitated and frowned, "not exactly. I mean, I suppose he could have looked through them at any time if he liked, but he wouldn't be . . ."

Inspector Neele finished the sentence for him.

"Wouldn't be supposed to do so?"

Lance grinned broadly. "That's right. Frankly, it would have been snooping. But Percy, I should imagine, always did snoop."

Inspector Neele nodded. He, also, thought it probable that Percival Fortescue snooped. It would be in keeping with what the Inspector was beginning to learn of his character.

"And talk of the devil," murmured Lance, as at that moment the door opened and Percival Fortescue came in. About to speak to the Inspector, he stopped, frowning, as he saw Lance.

"Hallo," he said. "You here? You didn't tell me you were coming here today."

"I felt a kind of zeal for work coming over me," said Lance, "so here I am ready to make myself useful. What do you want me to do?"

Percival said testily, "Nothing at present. Nothing at all. We shall have to come to some kind of arrangement as to what side of the business you're going to look after. We shall have to arrange an office for you."

Lance inquired, with a grin:

"By the way, why did you get rid of glamorous Grosvenor, old boy, and replace her by Horse-faced Hetty out there?"

"Really, Lance," Percival protested sharply.

"Definitely a change for the worse," said Lance. "I've been looking forward to the glamorous Grosvenor. Why did you sack her? Thought she knew a bit too much?"

"Of course not. What an idea!" Percy spoke angrily, a flush mounting his pale face. He turned to the Inspector. "You mustn't pay any attention to my brother," he said coldly. "He has a rather peculiar sense of humor." He added, "I never had a very high opinion of Miss Grosvenor's intelligence. Mrs. Hardcastle has excellent references and is most capable, besides very moderate in her terms."

"Very moderate in her terms," murmured Lance, casting his eyes towards the ceiling. "You know, Percy, I don't really approve of skimping over the office personnel. By the way, considering how loyally the staff has stood by us during these last tragic weeks, don't you think we ought to raise their salaries all round?"

"Certainly not," snapped Percival Fortescue. "Quite uncalled for and unnecessary."

Inspector Neele noticed the gleam of devilry in Lance's eyes. Percival, however, was far too upset to notice it.

"You always had the most extraordinarily extravagant ideas," he stuttered. "In the state in which this firm has been left, economy is our only hope."

Inspector Neele coughed apologetically.

"That's one of the things I wanted to talk to you about, Mr. Fortescue," he said to Percival.

"Yes, Inspector?" Percival switched his attention to Neele.

"I want to put certain suggestions before you, Mr. Fortescue. I understand that for the past six months or longer, possibly a year, your father's general behavior and conduct have been a source of increasing anxiety to you."

"He wasn't well," said Percival with finality. "He certainly wasn't at all well."

"You tried to induce him to see a doctor but you failed. He refused categorically?"

"That is so."

"May I ask you if you suspected that your father was suffering from what is familiarly referred to as G.P.I., General Paralysis of the Insane, a condition with signs of megalomania and irritability, which terminates sooner or later in hopeless insanity?"

Percival looked surprised. "It is remarkably astute of you, Inspector. That is exactly what I did fear. That is why I was so anxious for my father to submit to medical treatment."

Neele went on:

"In the meantime, until you could persuade your father to do that, he was capable of causing great havoc to the business?"

"He certainly was," Percival agreed.

"A very unfortunate state of affairs," said the Inspector.

"Quite terrible. No one knows the anxiety I have been through."

Neele said gently, "From the business point of view, your father's death was an extremely fortunate circumstance."

Percival said sharply, "You can hardly think I would regard my father's death in that light."

"It is not a question of how you regard it, Mr. Fortescue. I'm speaking merely of a question of fact. Your father died before his finances were completely on the rocks."

Percival said impatiently, "Yes, yes. As a matter of actual fact, you are right."

"It was a fortunate occurrence for your whole family, since they are dependent on this business."

"Yes. But really, Inspector, I don't see what you're driving at . . ." Percival broke off.

"Oh, I'm not driving at anything, Mr. Fortescue," said Neele. "I just like getting my facts straight. Now, there's another thing. I understood you to say that you'd had no communication of any kind with your brother here since he left England many years ago."

"Quite so," said Percival.

"Yes, but it isn't quite so, is it, Mr. Fortescue? I mean that last summer when you were so worried about your father's health, you actually wrote to your brother in Africa, told him of your anxiety about your father's behavior. You wanted, I think, your brother to combine with you in getting your father medically examined and put under restraint, if necessary."

"I—I—really, I don't see . . ."

Percival was badly shaken.

"That is so, isn't it, Mr. Fortescue?"

"Well, actually, I thought it only right. After all, Lancelot was a junior partner."

Inspector Neele transferred his gaze to Lance. Lance was grinning.

"You received that letter?" Inspector Neele asked.

Lance Fortescue nodded.

"What did you reply to it?"

Lance's grin widened.

"I told Percy to go and boil his head and to let the old man alone. I said the old man probably knew what he was doing quite well."

Inspector Neele's gaze went back again to Percival.

"Were those the terms of your brother's answer?"

"I—I—well, I suppose roughly, yes. Far more offensively couched, however."

"I thought the Inspector had better have a bowdlerized version," said Lance. He went on, "Frankly, Inspector Neele, that is one of the reasons why, when I got a letter from my father, I came home to see for myself what I thought. In the short interview I had with my father, frankly, I couldn't see anything much wrong with him. He was slightly excitable, that was all. He appeared to me perfectly capable of managing his own affairs. Anyway, after I got back to Africa and had talked things over with Pat, I decided that I'd come home and—what shall we say?—see fair play."

He shot a glance at Percival as he spoke.

"I object," said Percival Fortescue. "I object strongly to what you are suggesting. I was not intending to victimize my father. I was concerned for his health. I admit that I was also concerned . . ." he paused.

Lance filled the pause quickly.

"You were also concerned for your pocket, eh? For Percy's little pocket." He got up and all of a sudden his manner changed. "All right, Percy, I'm through. I was going to string you along a bit by pretending to work here. I wasn't going to let you have things all your own sweet way, but I'm damned if I'm going on with it. Frankly, it makes me sick to be in the same room with you. You've always been a dirty, mean, little skunk all your life. Prying and snooping and lying and making trouble. I'll tell you another thing. I can't prove it, but I've always believed it was you who forged that check there was all the row about, that got me shot out of here. For one thing, it was a damn bad forgery, a forgery that drew attention to itself in letters a foot high. My record was too bad for me to be able to protest effectively, but I often wondered that the old boy didn't realize that if I had forged his name I could have made a much better job of it than that."

Lance swept on, his voice rising, "Well, Percy, I'm

not going on with the silly game. I'm sick of this country, and of the City. I'm sick of little men like you with their pinstripe trousers and their black coats and their mincing voices and their mean, shoddy, financial deals. We'll share out as you suggested, and I'll get back with Pat to a different country—a country where there's room to breathe and move about. You can make your own list of securities. Keep the gilt-edged and the conservative ones, keep the safe 2 per cent and 3 per cent and 3½ percent. Give me father's latest wildcat speculations, as you call them. Most of them are probably duds. But I'll bet that one or two of them will pay better in the end than all your playing safe with 3 per cent Trustee stocks will do. Father was a shrewd old devil. He took chances, plenty of them. Some of those chances paid five and six and 700 per cent. I'll back his judgment and his luck. As for you, you little worm . . ."

Lance advanced towards his brother, who retreated rapidly round the end of the desk towards Inspector Neele. "All right," said Lance, "I'm not going to touch you. You wanted me out of here, you're getting me out of here. You ought to be satisfied." He added as he strode towards the door, "You can throw in the old Blackbird Mine concession too, if you like. If you've got the murdering MacKenzies on our trail, I'll draw them off to Africa." He added, as he swung through the doorway, "Revenge—after all these years—scarcely seems credible. But Inspector Neele seems to take it seriously, don't you, Inspector?"

"Nonsense," said Percival. "Such a thing is impossible!"

"Ask him," said Lance. "Ask him why he's making all these inquiries into blackbirds and rye in father's pocket."

Gently stroking his upper lip, Inspector Neele said, "You remember the blackbirds last summer, Mr. Fortescue. There are certain grounds for inquiry."

"Nonsense," said Percival again. "Nobody's heard of the MacKenzies for years."

"And yet," said Lance, "I'd almost dare to swear that there's a MacKenzie in our midst. I rather imagine the Inspector thinks so, too."

ii.

Inspector Neele caught up Lancelot Fortescue as the latter emerged into the street below.

Lance grinned at him rather sheepishly.

"I didn't mean to do that," he said. "But I suddenly lost my temper. Oh, well, it would have come to the same before long. I'm meeting Pat at the Savoy. Are you coming my way, Inspector?"

"No, I'm returning to Baydon Heath. But there's just something I'd like to ask you, Mr. Fortescue."

"Yes?"

"When you came into the inner office and saw me there, you were surprised. Why?"

"Because I didn't expect to see you, I suppose. I thought I'd find Percy there."

"You weren't told that he'd gone out?"

Lance looked at him curiously.

"No. They said he was in his office."

"I see. Nobody knew he'd gone out. There's no second door out of the inner office, but there is a door leading straight into the corridor from the little antechamber. I suppose your brother went out that way, but I'm surprised Mrs. Hardcastle didn't tell you so."

Lance laughed.

"She'd probably been to collect her cup of tea."

"Yes, yes—quite so."

Lance looked at him. "What's the idea, Inspector?"

"Just puzzling over a few little things, that's all, Mr. Fortescue."

Chapter Twenty-four

In the train on the way down to Baydon Heath, Inspector Neele had singularly little success doing the *Times* crossword. His mind was distracted by various possibilities. In the same way, he read the news with only half his brain taking it in. He read of an earthquake in Japan, of the discovery of uranium deposits in Tanganyika, of the body of a merchant seaman washed up near Southampton, and of the imminent strike among the dockers. He read of the latest victims of the cosh and of a new drug that had achieved wonders in advanced cases of tuberculosis.

All these items made a queer kind of pattern in the back of his mind. Presently he returned to the crossword puzzle and was able to put down three clues in rapid succession.

When he reached Yewtree Lodge he had come to a certain decision. He said to Sergeant Hay, "Where's that old lady? Is she still here?"

"Miss Marple? Oh, yes, she's here still. Great buddies with the old lady upstairs."

"I see." Neele paused for a moment and then said, "Where is she now? I'd like to see her."

Miss Marple arrived in a few minutes' time, looking rather flushed, and breathing fast.

"You want to see me, Inspector Neele? I do hope I haven't kept you waiting. Sergeant Hay couldn't find me at first. I was in the kitchen, talking to Mrs. Crump. I was congratulating her on her pastry and how light her hand is, and telling her how delicious the soufflé was last night. I always think, you know, it's better to approach a subject gradually, don't you? At least, I suppose it isn't so easy for you. You more or less have to come almost straightaway to the questions you want to ask. But, of course, for an old lady like me who has all the time in the world, as you might say, it's really expected of her that there should be a great deal of unnecessary talk. And the way to a cook's heart, as they say, is through her pastry."

"What you really wanted to talk to her about," said Inspector Neele, "was Gladys Martin."

Miss Marple nodded.

"Yes. Gladys. You see, Mrs. Crump could really tell me a lot about the girl. Not in connection with the murder. I don't mean that. But about her spirits lately and the odd things she said. I don't mean odd in the sense of peculiar. I mean just the odds and ends of conversation."

"Did you find it helpful?" asked Inspector Neele.

"Yes," said Miss Marple. "I found it very helpful indeed. I really think, you know, that things are becoming very much clearer, don't you?"

"I do and I don't," said Inspector Neele.

Sergeant Hay, he noticed, had left the room. He was

glad of it because what he was about to do and say now was, to say the least of it, slightly unorthodox.

"Look here, Miss Marple," he said, "I want to talk to you seriously."

"Yes, Inspector Neele?"

"In a way," said Inspector Neele, "you and I represent different points of view. I admit, Miss Marple, that I've heard something about you at the Yard." He said, "It seems you're fairly well known there."

"I don't know how it is," fluttered Miss Marple, "but I so often seem to get mixed up in things that are really no concern of mine. Crimes, I mean, and peculiar happenings."

"You've got a reputation," said Inspector Neele.

"Sir Henry Clithering, of course," said Miss Marple, "is a very old friend of mine."

"As I said before," Neele went on, "you and I represent opposite points of view. One might almost call them sanity and insanity."

Miss Marple put her head a little on one side.

"Now what exactly do you mean by that, I wonder, Inspector?"

"Well, Miss Marple, there's a sane way of looking at things. This murder benefits certain people. One person, I may say, in particular. The second murder benefits the same person. The third murder one might call a murder for safety."

"But which do you call the third murder?" Miss Marple asked.

Her eyes, a very bright china blue, looked shrewdly at the Inspector. He nodded.

"Yes. You've got something there, perhaps. You know, the other day when the A.C. was speaking to me of these murders, something that he said seemed to me to be wrong. That was it. I was thinking, of course, of the nursery rhyme. The king in his counting house, the queen in the parlor and the maid hanging out the clothes."

"Exactly," said Miss Marple. "A sequence in that order, but actually Gladys must have been murdered before Mrs. Fortescue, mustn't she?"

"I think so," said Neele. "I take it it's quite certainly so. Her body wasn't discovered till late that night, and of course it was difficult then to say exactly how long she'd been dead. But I think myself that she must almost certainly have been murdered round about five o'clock, because otherwise . . ."

Miss Marple cut in. "Because otherwise she would certainly have taken the second tray into the drawing-room?"

"Quite so. She took one tray in with the tea on it, she brought the second tray into the hall, and then something happened. She saw something or she heard something. The question is what that something was. It might have been Dubois coming down the stairs from Mrs. Fortescue's room. It might have been Elaine Fortescue's young man, Gerald Wright, coming in at the side door. Whoever it was lured her away from the tea tray and out into the garden. And once that had happened, I don't see any possibility of her death being long delayed. It was cold out and she was wearing only her thin uniform."

"Of course you're quite right," said Miss Marple. "I mean it was never a case of 'the maid was in the garden hanging up the clothes.' She wouldn't be hanging up clothes at that time of the evening and she wouldn't go out to the clothesline without putting a coat on. That was all camouflage, like the clothes peg, to make the thing fit in with the rhyme."

"Exactly," said Inspector Neele, "crazy. That's where I can't yet see eye to eye with you. I can't—I simply can't swallow this nursery rhyme business."

"But it fits, Inspector. You must agree it fits."

"It fits," said Neele heavily, "but all the same the sequence is wrong. I mean the rhyme definitely suggests that the maid was the third murder. But we know that the Queen was the third murder. Adele Fortescue was not killed until between twenty-five past five and five minutes to six. By then Gladys must already have been dead."

"And that's all wrong, isn't it?" said Miss Marple. "All wrong for the nursery rhyme—that's very significant, isn't it?"

Inspector Neele shrugged his shoulders.

"It's probably splitting hairs. The deaths fulfill the conditions of the rhyme, and I suppose that's all that was needed. But I'm talking now as though I were on your side. I'm going to outline my side of the case now, Miss Marple. I'm washing out the blackbirds and the rye and all the rest of it. I'm going by sober facts and common sense and the reasons for which sane people do murders. First, the death of Rex Fortescue, and whom his death benefits. Well, it benefits quite a lot of people, but most of all it benefits his son, Percival. His son Percival wasn't at Yewtree Lodge that morning. He couldn't have put poison in his father's coffee or in anything that he ate for breakfast. Or that's what we thought at first."

"Ah," Miss Marple's eyes brightened. "So there was a method, was there? I've been thinking about it, you know, a good deal, and I've had several ideas. But, of course, no evidence or proof."

"There's no harm in my letting you know," said Inspector Neele. "Taxine was added to a new jar of marmalade. That jar of marmalade was placed on the breakfast table and the top layer of it was eaten by Mr. Fortescue at breakfast. Later that jar of marmalade was thrown out into the bushes and a similar jar with a similar amount taken out of it was placed in the pantry. The jar in the bushes was found, and I've just had the result of the analysis. It shows definite evidence of taxine."

"So that was it," murmured Miss Marple. "So simple and easy to do."

"Consolidated Investments," Neele went on, "was in a bad way. If the firm had had to pay out a hundred thousand pounds to Adele Fortescue under her husband's will, it would, I think, have crashed. If Mrs. Fortescue had survived her husband for a month, that money would have had to be paid out to her. She would have had no feeling for the firm or its difficulties. But she didn't survive her husband for a month. She died, and as a result of her death the gainer was the residuary legatee of Rex Fortescue's will. In other words, Percival Fortescue again.

"Always Percival Fortescue," the Inspector continued bitterly. "And though he could have tampered with the marmalade, he couldn't have poisoned his stepmother or strangled Gladys. According to his secretary, he was in his city office at five o'clock that afternoon, and he didn't arrive back here until nearly seven."

"That makes it very difficult, doesn't it?" said Miss Marple.

"It makes it impossible," said Inspector Neele gloomily. "In other words, Percival is out." Abandoning restraint and prudence, he spoke with some bitterness, almost unaware of his listener. "Wherever I go, wherever I turn, I always come up against the same person. Percival Fortescue! Yet it can't be Percival Fortescue." Calming himself a little he said, "Oh, there are other possibilities, other people who had a perfectly good motive."

"Mr. Dubois, of course," said Miss Marple sharply.

"And that young Mr. Wright. I do so agree with you, Inspector. Wherever there is a question of gain, one has to be very suspicious. The great thing to avoid is having in any way a trustful mind."

In spite of himself, Neele smiled.

"Always think the worst, eh?" he asked.

It seemed a curious doctrine to be proceeding from this charming and fragile-looking old lady.

"Oh yes," said Miss Marple fervently. "I always believe the worst. What is so sad is that one is usually justified in doing so."

"All right," said Neele, "let's think the worst. Dubois could have done it, Gerald Wright could have done it (that is to say, if he'd been acting in collusion with Elaine Fortescue and she tampered with the marmalade), Mrs. Percival could have done it, I suppose. She was on the spot. But none of the people I have mentioned tie up with the crazy angle. They don't tie up with blackbirds and pockets full of rye. That's your theory and it may be that you're right. If so, it boils down to one person, doesn't it? Mrs. MacKenzie's in a mental home and has been for a good number of years. She hasn't been messing about with marmalade pots or putting cyanide in the drawing-room afternoon tea. Her son Donald was killed at Dunkirk. That leaves the daughter Ruby MacKenzie. And if your theory is correct, if this whole series of murders arises out of the old Blackbird Mine business, then Ruby MacKenzie must be here in this house, and there's only one person that Ruby MacKenzie could be."

"I think, you know," said Miss Marple, "that you're being a little too dogmatic."

Inspector Neele paid no attention.

"Just one person," he said grimly.

He got up and went out of the room.

ii.

Mary Dove was in her own sitting room. It was a small, rather austerely furnished room, but comfortable. When Inspector Neele tapped at the door, Mary Dove raised her head, which had been bent over a pile of tradesmen's books, and said in her clear voice:

"Come in."

The Inspector entered.

"Do sit down, Inspector." Miss Dove indicated a chair. "Could you wait just one moment? The total of the fishmonger's account does not seem to be correct, and I must check it."

Inspector Neele sat in silence, watching her as she totted up the column. How wonderfully calm and self-possessed the girl was, he thought. He was intrigued, as so often before, by the personality that underlay that self-assured manner. He tried to trace in her features any resemblance to those of the woman he had talked to at the Pinewood Sanatorium. The coloring was not unlike, but he could detect no real facial resemblance. Presently Mary Dove raised her head from her accounts and said:

"Yes, Inspector? What can I do for you?"

Inspector Neele said quietly. "You know, Miss Dove, there are certain very peculiar features about this case."

"Yes?"

"To begin with, there is the odd circumstance of the rye found in Mr. Fortescue's pocket."

"That was very extraordinary," Mary Dove agreed. "You know, I really cannot think of any explanation for that."

"Then there is the curious circumstance of the blackbirds. Those four blackbirds on Mr. Fortescue's desk last summer, and also the incident of the blackbirds being substituted for the veal and ham in the pie. You were here, I think, Miss Dove, at the time of both those occurrences?"

"Yes, I was. I remember now. It was most upsetting. It seemed such a very purposeless, spiteful thing to do, especially at the time."

"Perhaps not entirely purposeless. What do you know, Miss Dove, about the Blackbird Mine?"

"I don't think I've ever heard of the Blackbird Mine."

"Your name, you told me, is Mary Dove. Is that your real name, Miss Dove?"

Mary Dove raised her eyebrows. Inspector Neele was almost sure that a wary expression had come into her blue eyes.

"What an extraordinary question, Inspector. Are you suggesting that my name is not Mary Dove?"

"That is exactly what I am suggesting. I'm suggesting," said Neele pleasantly, "that your name is Ruby MacKenzie."

She stared at him. For a moment her face was entirely blank, with neither protest on it nor surprise. There was, Inspector Neele thought, a very definite effect of calculation. After a minute or two she said in a quiet, colorless voice, "What do you expect me to say?"

"Please answer me. Is your name Ruby MacKenzie?"

"I have told you my name is Mary Dove."

"Yes, but have you proof of that, Miss Dove?"

"What do you want to see? My birth certificate?"

"That might be helpful or it might not. You might, I mean, be in possession of the birth certificate of a Mary Dove. That Mary Dove might be a friend of yours or might be someone who had died."

"Yes, there are a lot of possibilities, aren't there?" Amusement had crept back into Mary Dove's voice. "It's really quite a dilemma for you, isn't it, Inspector?"

"They might possibly be able to recognize you at Pinewood Sanatorium," said Neele.

"Pinewood Sanatorium!" Mary raised her eyebrows. "What or where is Pinewood Sanatorium?"

"I think you know very well, Miss Dove."

"I assure you I am quite in the dark."

"And you deny categorically that you are Ruby Mac-Kenzie?"

"I shouldn't really like to deny anything. I think, you know, Inspector, that it's up to you to prove I am this Ruby MacKenzie, whoever she is." There was definite amusement now in her blue eyes, amusement and challenge. Looking him straight in the eyes, Mary Dove said, "Yes, it's up to you, Inspector. Prove that I'm Ruby MacKenzie, if you can."

Chapter Twenty-five

"The old tabby's looking for you, sir," said Sergeant Hay in a conspiratorial whisper, as Inspector Neele descended the stairs. "It appears as how she's got a lot more to say to you."

"Hell and damnation," said Inspector Neele.

"Yes, sir," said Sergeant Hay, not a muscle of his face moving.

He was about to move away when Neele called him back.

"Go over those notes given us by Miss Dove, Hay, notes as to her former employment and situations. Check up on them—and, yes, there are just one or two other things that I would like to know. Put these inquiries in hand, will you?"

He jotted down a few lines on a sheet of paper and gave them to Sergeant Hay who said, "I'll get on to it at once, sir."

Hearing a murmur of voices in the library as he

passed, Inspector Neele looked in. Whether Miss Marple had been looking for him or not, she was now fully engaged talking to Mrs. Percival Fortescue while her knitting needles clicked busily. The middle of the sentence which Inspector Neele caught was:

". . . I have really always thought it was a vocation you needed for nursing. It certainly is very noble work."

Inspector Neele withdrew quietly. Miss Marple had noticed him, he thought, but she had taken no notice of his presence.

She went on in her gentle, soft voice:

"I had such a charming nurse looking after me when I once broke my wrist. She went on from me to nurse Mrs. Sparrow's son, a very nice young naval officer. Quite a romance, really, because they became engaged. So romantic I thought it. They were married and were very happy and had two dear little children." Miss Marple sighed sentimentally. "It was pneumonia, you know. So much depends on nursing in pneumonia, does it not?"

"Oh, yes," said Jennifer Fortescue, "nursing is nearly everything in pneumonia, though, of course, nowadays M and B Sulfa works wonders, and it's not the long, protracted battle it used to be."

"I'm sure you must have been an excellent nurse, my dear," said Miss Marple. "That was the beginning of your romance, was it not? I mean, you came here to nurse Mr. Percival Fortescue, did you not?"

"Yes," said Jennifer. "Yes, yes—that's how it did happen."

Her voice was not encouraging, but Miss Marple seemed to take no notice.

"I understand. One should not listen to servants' gossip, of course, but I'm afraid an old lady like myself is always interested to hear about the people in the house. Now, what was I saying? Oh, yes. There was another nurse at first, was there not? and she got sent away—something like that. Carelessness, I believe."

"I don't think it was carelessness," said Jennifer. "I believe her father or someone was desperately ill, and so I came to replace her."

"I see," said Miss Marple. "And you fell in love and that was that. Yes, very nice indeed, very nice."

"I'm not so sure about that," said Jennifer Fortescue. "I often wish," her voice trembled, "I often wish I was back in the wards again."

"Yes, yes, I understand. You were keen on your profession."

"I wasn't so much at the time, but now when I think of it—life's so monotonous, you know. Day after day with nothing to do, and Val so absorbed in business."

Miss Marple shook her head.

"Gentlemen have to work so hard nowadays," she said. "There really doesn't seem any leisure, no matter how much money there is."

"Yes, it makes it very lonely and dull for a wife sometimes. I often wish I'd never come here," said Jennifer. "Oh, well, I dare say it serves me right. I ought never to have done it."

"Ought never to have done what, my dear?"

"I ought never to have married Val. Oh, well—" she sighed abruptly. "Don't let's talk of it any more."

Obligingly, Miss Marple began to talk about the new skirts that were being worn in Paris.

ii.

"So kind of you not to interrupt just now," said Miss Marple when, having tapped at the door of the study, Inspector Neele had told her to come in. "There were just one or two little points, you know, that I wanted to verify." She added reproachfully, "We didn't really finish our little talk just now."

"I'm so sorry, Miss Marple." Inspector Neele summoned up a charming smile. "I'm afraid I was rather rude. I summoned you to a consultation and did all the talking myself."

"Oh, that's quite all right," said Miss Marple immediately, "because, you see, I wasn't really quite ready then to put all my cards on the table. I mean, I wouldn't like to make any accusation unless I was absolutely sure about it. Sure, that is, in my own mind. And I am sure, now."

"You're sure about what, Miss Marple?"

"Well, certainly about who killed Mr. Fortescue. What you told me about the marmalade, I mean, just clinches the matter. Showing how, I mean, as well as who, and well within the mental capacity."

Inspector Neele blinked a little.

"I'm so sorry," said Miss Marple, perceiving this reaction on his part. "I'm afraid I find it difficult sometimes to make myself perfectly clear."

"I'm not quite sure yet, Miss Marple, what we're talking about."

"Well, perhaps," said Miss Marple, "we'd better begin all over again. I mean, if you could spare the time. I would rather like to put my own point of view before you. You see, I've talked a good deal to people, to old Miss Ramsbottom and to Mrs. Crump and to her husband. He, of course, is a liar, but that doesn't really matter because if you know liars are liars, it comes to the same thing. But I did want to get the telephone calls clear and the nylon stockings and all that."

Inspector Neele blinked again and wondered what he had let himself in for and why he had ever thought that Miss Marple might be a desirable and clear-headed colleague. Still, he thought to himself, however muddle-

headed she was, she might have picked up some useful
bits of information. All Inspector Neele's successes in
his profession had come from listening well. He was prepared to listen now.

"Please tell me all about it, Miss Marple," he said,
"but start at the beginning, won't you?"

"Yes, of course," said Miss Marple, "and the beginning is Gladys. I mean I came here because of Gladys.
And you very kindly let me look through all her things.
And what with that and the nylon stockings and the telephone calls and one thing and another, it did come out
perfectly clear. I mean about Mr. Fortescue and the
taxine."

"You have a theory," asked Inspector Neele, "as to
who put the taxine into Mr. Fortescue's marmalade?"

"It isn't a theory," said Miss Marple. "I know."

For the third time Inspector Neele blinked.

"It was Gladys, of course," said Miss Marple.

Chapter Twenty-six

Inspector Neele stared at Miss Marple and slowly shook his head.

"Are you saying," he said incredulously, "that Gladys Martin deliberately murdered Rex Fortescue? I'm sorry, Miss Marple, but I simply don't believe it."

"No, of course she didn't mean to murder him," said Miss Marple, "but she did it all the same! You said yourself that she was nervous and upset when you questioned her. And that she looked guilty."

"Yes, but not guilty of murder."

"Oh, no, I agree. As I say, she didn't mean to murder anybody, but she put the taxine in the marmalade. She didn't think it was poison, of course."

"What did she think it was?" Inspector Neele's voice still sounded incredulous.

"I rather imagine she thought it was a truth drug," said Miss Marple. "It's very interesting, you know, and

very instructive—the things these girls cut out of papers
and keep. It's always been the same, you know, all
through the ages. Recipes for beauty, for attracting the
man you love. And witchcraft and charms and marvel-
ous happenings. Nowadays they're mostly lumped together under the heading of Science. Nobody believes in
magicians any more, nobody believes that anyone can
come along and wave a wand and turn you into a frog.
But if you read in the paper that by injecting certain
glands scientists can alter your vital tissues and you'll
develop froglike characteristics, well, everybody would
believe that. And having read in the papers about truth
drugs, of course Gladys would believe it absolutely
when he told her that that's what it was."

"When who told her?" asked Inspector Neele.

"Albert Evans," said Miss Marple. "Not, of course,
that that is really his name. But, anyway, he met her
last summer at a holiday camp, and he flattered her up
and made love to her, and I should imagine, told her
some story of injustice or persecution, or something like
that. Anyway, the point was that Rex Fortescue had
to be made to confess what he had done and make
restitution. I don't know this, of course, Inspector
Neele, but I'm pretty sure about it. He got her to take
a post here, and it's really very easy nowadays, with the
shortage of domestic staff, to obtain a post where you
want one. Staffs are changing the whole time. Then they
arranged a date together. You remember on that last
post card he said, 'Remember our date.' That was to be
the great day they were working for. Gladys would put
the drug that he gave her into the top of the marmalade,
so that Mr. Fortescue would eat it at breakfast, and she
would also put the rye in his pocket. I don't know what
story he told her to account for the rye, but as I told
you from the beginning, Inspector Neele, Gladys Martin
was a very credulous girl. In fact, there's hardly any-

thing she wouldn't believe if a personable young man put it to her the right way."

"Go on," said Inspector Neele in a dazed voice.

"The idea probably was," continued Miss Marple, "that Albert was going to call upon him at the office that day, and that by that time the truth drug would have worked, and that Mr. Fortescue would have confessed everything and so on and so on. You can imagine the poor girl's feelings when she hears that Mr. Fortescue is dead."

"But, surely," Inspector Neele objected, "she would have told?"

Miss Marple asked sharply, "What was the first thing she said to you when you questioned her?"

"She said 'I didn't do it,'" Inspector Neele said.

"Exactly," said Miss Marple triumphantly. "Don't you see that's exactly what she would say? If she broke an ornament, you know, Gladys would always say, 'I didn't do it, Miss Marple. I can't think how it happened.' They can't help it, poor dears. They're very upset at what they've done and their great idea is to avoid blame. You don't think that a nervous young woman who had murdered someone when she didn't mean to murder him is going to admit it, do you? That would have been quite out of character."

"Yes," Neele said, "I suppose it would."

He ran his mind back over his interview with Gladys. Nervous, upset, guilty, shifty-eyed, all those things. They might have had small significance or a big one. He could not really blame himself for having failed to come to the right conclusion.

"Her first idea, as I say," went on Miss Marple, "would be to deny it all. Then, in a confused way, she would try to sort it all out in her mind. Perhaps Albert hadn't known how strong the stuff was, or he'd made a mistake and given her too much of it. She'd think of excuses for him and explanations. She'd hope he'd get in touch with her, which, of course, he did. By telephone."

"Do you know that?" asked Neele sharply.

Miss Marple shook her head.

"No. I admit I'm assuming it. But there were calls that day. That is to say, people rang up, and when Crump, or Mrs. Crump answered, the phone was hung up. That's what he'd do, you know. Ring up and wait until Gladys answered the phone, and then he'd make an appointment with her to meet him."

"I see," said Neele. "You mean she had an appointment to meet him on the day she died."

Miss Marple nodded vigorously.

"Yes, that was indicated. Mrs. Crump was right about one thing. The girl had on her best nylon stockings and her good shoes. She was going to meet someone. Only, she wasn't going out to meet him. He was coming to Yewtree Lodge. That's why she was on the lookout that day and flustered and late with tea. Then, as she brought the second tray into the hall, I think she looked along the passage to the side door, and saw him there, beckoning to her. She put the tray down and went out to meet him."

"And then he strangled her," said Neele.

Miss Marple pursed her lips together. "It would only take a minute," she said, "but he couldn't risk her talking. She had to die, poor, silly, credulous girl. And then —he put a clothes peg on her nose!" Stern anger vibrated the old lady's voice. "To make it fit in with the rhyme. The rye, the blackbirds, the counting house, the bread and honey, and the clothes peg—the nearest he could get to a little dickey bird that nipped off her nose."

"And I suppose at the end of it all he'll go to Broadmoor, and we shan't be able to hang him because he's crazy!" said Neele slowly.

"I think you'll hang him all right," said Miss Marple. "And he's not crazy, Inspector, not for a moment!"

Inspector Neele looked hard at her.

"Now see here, Miss Marple, you've outlined a theory to me. Yes, yes—although you say you know, it's only a theory. You're saying that a man is responsible for these crimes, who called himself Albert Evans, who picked up the girl Gladys at a holiday camp and used her for his own purposes. This Albert Evans was someone who wanted revenge for the old Blackbird Mine business. You're suggesting, aren't you, that Mrs. MacKenzie's son, Don MacKenzie, didn't die at Dunkirk. That he's still alive, that he's behind all this?"

But to Inspector Neele's surprise, Miss Marple was shaking her head violently.

"Oh no!" she said, "oh no! I'm not suggesting that at all. Don't you see, Inspector Neele, all this blackbird business is really a complete fake? It was used, that was all, used by somebody who heard about the blackbirds —the ones in the library and in the pie. The blackbirds were genuine enough. They were put there by someone who knew about the old business, who wanted revenge for it. But only the revenge of trying to frighten Mr. Fortescue or to make him uncomfortable. I don't believe, you know, Inspector Neele, that children can really be brought up and taught to wait and brood and carry out revenge. Children, after all, have got a lot of sense. But anyone whose father had been swindled and perhaps left to die might be willing to play a malicious trick on the person who was supposed to have done it. That's what happened, I think. And the killer used it."

"The killer," said Inspector Neele. "Come now, Miss Marple, let's have your ideas about the killer. Who was he?"

"You won't be surprised," said Miss Marple. "Not really. Because you'll see, as soon as I tell you who he is or rather who I think he is, for one must be accurate, must one not? You'll see that he's just the type of person who would commit these murders. He's sane, brilliant and quite unscrupulous. And he did it, of course, for money, probably for a good deal of money."

"Percival Fortescue?" Inspector Neele spoke almost imploringly, but he knew as he spoke that he was wrong. The picture of the man that Miss Marple had built up for him had no resemblance to Percival Fortescue.

"Oh, no," said Miss Marple. "Not Percival. Lance."

Chapter Twenty-seven

"It's impossible," said Inspector Neele.

He leaned back in his chair and watched Miss Marple with fascinated eyes. As Miss Marple had said, he was not surprised. His words were a denial not of probability, but of possibility. Lance Fortescue fitted the description: Miss Marple had outlined it well enough. But Inspector Neele simply could not see how Lance could be the answer.

Miss Marple leaned forward in her chair and gently, persuasively, and rather in the manner of someone explaining the simple facts of arithmetic to a small child, outlined her theory.

"He's always been like that, you see. I mean, he's always been bad. Bad all through, although with it he's always been attractive. Especially attractive to women. He's got a brilliant mind and he'll take risks. He's always taken risks, and because of his charm people have always believed the best and not the worst about him. He came home in the summer to see his father. I don't believe for a moment that his father wrote to him or sent for him—unless, of course, you've got actual evidence to that effect." She paused inquiringly.

Neele shook his head. "No," he said, "I've no evidence of his father sending for him. I've got a letter that Lance is supposed to have written to him. But Lance could quite easily have slipped that among his father's papers in the study here the day he arrived."

"Sharp of him," said Miss Marple, nodding her head. "Well, as I say, he probably flew over here and attempted a reconciliation with his father, but Mr. Fortescue wouldn't have it. You see, Lance had recently got married, and the small pittance he was living on, and which he had doubtless been supplementing in various dishonest ways, was not enough for him any more. He was very much in love with Pat (who is a dear, sweet girl) and he wanted a respectable, settled life with her—nothing shifty. And that, from his point of view, meant having a lot of money. When he was at Yewtree Lodge, he must have heard about these blackbirds. Perhaps his father mentioned them. Perhaps Adele did. He jumped to the conclusion that MacKenzie's daughter was established in the house, and it occurred to him that she would make a very good scapegoat for murder. Because, you see, when he realized that he couldn't get his father to do what he wanted, he must have cold-bloodedly decided that murder it would have to be. He may have realized that his father wasn't—er—very well—and have feared that by the time his father died there would have been a complete crash."

"He knew about his father's health all right," said the Inspector.

"Ah—that explains a good deal. Perhaps the coincidence of his father's Christian name being Rex together with the blackbird incident suggested the idea of the nursery rhyme. Make a crazy business of the whole thing—and tie it up with that old revenge threat of the MacKenzies. Then, you see, he could dispose of Adele, too, and that hundred thousand pounds going out of the firm. But there would have to be a third character, the 'maid in the garden hanging up the clothes'—and I suppose that suggested the whole wicked plan to him. An innocent accomplice whom he could silence before she could talk. And that would give him what he wanted —a genuine alibi for the first murder.

"The rest was easy. He arrived here from the station just before five o'clock, which was the time when Gladys brought the second tray into the hall. He came to the side door, saw her and beckoned to her. Strangling her and carrying her body round the house to where the clotheslines were would only have taken three or four minutes. Then he rang the front doorbell, was admitted to the house, and joined the family for tea. After tea he went up to see Miss Ramsbottom. When he came down, he slipped into the drawing-room, found Adele alone there drinking a last cup of tea and sat down by her on the sofa, and while he was talking to her, he managed to slip the cyanide into her tea. It wouldn't be difficult, you know. A little piece of white stuff, like sugar. He might have stretched out his hand to the sugar basin and taken a lump and apparently dropped it into her cup. He'd laugh and say, 'Look, I've dropped more sugar into your tea.' She'd say she didn't mind, stir it and drink it. It would be as easy and audacious as that. Yes, he's an audacious fellow."

Inspector Neele said slowly, "It's actually possible— yes. But I cannot see—really, Miss Marple, I cannot see —what he stood to gain by it. Granted that unless old Fortescue died the business would soon be on the rocks, is Lance's share big enough to cause him to plan three murders? I don't think so. I really don't think so."

"That is a little difficult," admitted Miss Marple. "Yes, I agree with you. That does present difficulties. I suppose . . ." She hesitated, looking at the Inspector. "I suppose—I am so very ignorant in financial matters —but I suppose it is really true that the Blackbird Mine is worthless?"

Neele reflected. Various scraps fitted together in his mind. Lance's willingness to take the various speculative or worthless shares off Percival's hands. His parting words today in London that Percival had better get rid of the Blackbird and its hoodoo. A gold mine. A worthless gold mine. But perhaps the mine had not been worthless. And yet, somehow, that seemed unlikely. Old Rex Fortescue was hardly likely to have made a mistake on that point, although of course there might have been soundings recently. Where was the mine? West Africa, Lance had said. Yes, but somebody else—was it Miss Ramsbottom—had said it was in East Africa. Had Lance been deliberately misleading when he said West instead of East? Miss Ramsbottom was old and forgetful, and yet she might have been right and not Lance. East Africa. Lance had just come from East Africa. Had he perhaps some recent knowledge?

Suddenly with a click another piece fitted into the Inspector's puzzle. Sitting in the train, reading the *Times. Uranium deposits found in Tanganyika.* Supposing that the uranium deposits were on the site of the old Blackbird? That would explain everything. Lance had come to have knowledge of that, being on the spot, and with uranium deposits there, there was a fortune to be grasped. An enormous fortune! He sighed. He looked at Miss Marple.

"How do you think," he asked reproachfully, "that I'm ever going to be able to prove all this?"

Miss Marple nodded at him encouragingly as an aunt

might have encouraged a bright nephew who was going in for a scholarship exam.

"You'll prove it," she said. "You're a very, very clever man, Inspector Neele. I've seen that from the first. Now you know who it is, you ought to be able to get the evidence. At that holiday camp, for instance, they'll recognize his photograph. He'll find it hard to explain why he stayed there for a week calling himself Albert Evans."

Yes, Inspector Neele thought, Lance Fortescue was brilliant and unscrupulous, but he was foolhardy, too. The risks he took were just a little too great.

Neele thought to himself, "I'll get him!" Then, doubt sweeping over him, he looked at Miss Marple.

"It's all pure assumption, you know," he said.

"Yes—but you are sure, aren't you?"

"I suppose so. After all, I've known his kind before." The old lady nodded.

"Yes—that matters so much—that's really why I'm sure."

Neele looked at her playfully.

"Because of your knowledge of criminals."

"Oh, no, of course not. Because of Pat—a dear girl —and the kind that always marries a bad lot. That's really what drew my attention to him at the start."

"I may be sure—in my own mind," said the Inspector, "but there's a lot that needs explaining—the Ruby MacKenzie business for instance. I could swear that—"

Miss Marple interrupted, "And you're quite right. But you've been thinking of the wrong person. Go and talk to Mrs. Percy."

ii.

"Mrs. Fortescue," said Inspector Neele, "do you mind telling me your name before you were married?"

"Oh!" Jennifer gasped. She looked frightened.

"You needn't be nervous, madam," said Inspector Neele, "but it's much better to come out with the truth. I'm right, I think, in saying that your name before you were married was Ruby MacKenzie?"

"My—well, oh well—oh dear—well, why shouldn't it be?" said Mrs. Percival Fortescue.

"No reason at all," said Inspector Neele gently, and added, "I was talking to your mother a few days ago at Pinewood Sanatorium."

"She's very angry with me," said Jennifer. "I never go and see her now because it only upsets her. Poor Mumsy, she was so devoted to Dad, you know."

"And she brought you up to have very melodramatic ideas of revenge?"

"Yes," said Jennifer. "She kept making us swear on the Bible that we'd never forget and that we'd kill him one day. Of course, once I'd gone into hospital and started my training, I began to realize that her mental balance wasn't what it should be."

"You yourself must have felt revengeful though, Mrs. Fortescue?"

"Well, of course I did. Rex Fortescue practically murdered my father! I don't mean he actually shot him, or knifed him or anything like that. But I'm quite certain that he did leave Father to die. That's the same thing, isn't it?"

"It's the same thing morally—yes."

"So I did want to pay him back," said Jennifer. "When a friend of mine came to nurse his son I got her to leave and to propose my replacing her. I don't know exactly what I meant to do. . . . I didn't, really I didn't, Inspector, I never meant to kill Mr. Fortescue. I had some idea, I think, of nursing his son so badly that the son would die. But, of course, if you are a nurse by profession, you can't do that sort of thing. Actually, I had quite a job pulling Val through. And then he got fond of me and asked me to marry him and I thought, Well, really, that's a far more sensible revenge than anything else. I mean, to marry Mr. Fortescue's eldest son and get the money he swindled Father out of back that way. I think it was a far more sensible way."

"Yes, indeed," said Inspector Neele, "far more sensible." He added, "It was you, I suppose, who put the blackbirds on the desk and in the pie?"

Mrs. Percival flushed.

"Yes. I suppose it was silly of me really. . . . But Mr. Fortescue had been talking about suckers one day and boasting of how he'd swindled people—got the best of them. Oh, in quite a legal way. And I thought I'd just like to give him—well, a kind of fright. And it did give him a fright! He was awfully upset." She added anxiously, "But I didn't do anything else! I didn't really, Inspector. You don't—you don't honestly think I would murder anyone, do you?"

Inspector Neele smiled.

"No," he said, "I don't." He added, "By the way, have you given Miss Dove any money lately?"

Jennifer's jaw dropped.

"How did you know?"

"We know a lot of things," said Inspector Neele and added to himself, "And guess a good many, too."

Jeinfer continued, speaking rapidly.

"She came to me and said that you'd accused her of being Ruby MacKenzie. She said if I'd get hold of five hundred pounds she'd let you go on thinking so. She said if you knew that I was Ruby MacKenzie, I'd be suspected of murdering Mr. Fortescue and my step-mother. I had an awful job getting the money because, of course, I couldn't tell Percival. He doesn't know about me. I had to sell my diamond engagement ring and a very beautiful necklace Mr. Fortescue gave me."

"Don't worry, Mrs. Percival," said Inspector Neele, "I think we can get your money back for you."

iii.

It was on the following day that Inspector Neele had another interview with Miss Dove.

"I wonder, Miss Dove," he said, "if you'd give me a check for five hundred pounds payable to Mrs. Percival Fortescue."

He had the pleasure of seeing Mary Dove lose countenance for once.

"The silly fool told you, I suppose," she said.

"Yes. Blackmail, Miss Dove, is rather a serious charge."

"It wasn't exactly blackmail, Inspector. I think you'd find it hard to make out a case of blackmail against me. I was just doing Mrs. Percival a special service to oblige her."

"Well, if you'll give me that check, Miss Dove, we'll leave it like that."

Mary Dove got her checkbook and took out her fountain pen.

"It's very annoying," she said with a sigh. "I'm particularly hard up at the moment."

"You'll be looking for another job soon, I suppose?"

"Yes. This one hasn't turned out quite according to plan. It's all been very unfortunate from my point of view."

Inspector Neele agreed.

"Yes, it put you in rather a difficult position, didn't it? I mean, it was quite likely that any moment we might have to look into your antecedents."

Mary Dove, cool once more, allowed her eyebrows to rise.

"Really, Inspector, my past is quite blameless, I assure you."

"Yes, it is," Inspector Neele agreed cheerfully. "We've nothing against you at all, Miss Dove. It's a curious coincidence, though, that in the last three places which you have filled so admirably, there have happened to be robberies about three months after you left. The thieves have seemed remarkably well informed as to where mink coats, jewels, et cetera, were kept. Curious coincidence, isn't it?"

"Coincidences do happen, Inspector."

"Oh, yes," said Neele. "They happen. But they mustn't happen too often, Miss Dove. I dare say," he added, "that we may meet again in the future."

"I hope," said Mary Dove, "I don't mean to be rude, Inspector Neele—but I hope we don't."

Chapter Twenty-eight

Miss Marple smoothed over the top of her suitcase, tucked in an end of woolly shawl and shut the lid down. She looked round her bedroom. No, she had left nothing behind. Crump came in to fetch down her luggage. Miss Marple went into the next room to say good-by to Miss Ramsbottom.

"I'm afraid," said Miss Marple, "that I've made a very poor return for your hospitality. I hope you will be able to forgive me some day."

"Hah," said Miss Ramsbottom.

She was as usual playing patience.

"Black knave, red queen," she observed, then she darted a shrewd, sideways glance at Miss Marple. "You found out what you wanted to, I suppose," she said.

"Yes."

"And I suppose you've told that police inspector all about it? Will he be able to prove a case?"

235

"I'm almost sure he will," said Miss Marple. "It may take a little time."

"I'm not asking you any questions," said Miss Ramsbottom. "You're a shrewd woman. I knew that as soon as I saw you. I don't blame you for what you've done. Wickedness is wickedness and has got to be punished. There's a bad streak in this family. It didn't come from our side, I'm thankful to say. Elvira, my sister, was a fool. Nothing worse.

"Black knave," repeated Miss Ramsbottom, fingering the card. "Handsome, but a black heart. Yes, I was afraid of it. Ah, well, you can't always help loving a sinner. The boy always had a way with him. Even got round me. . . . Told a lie about the time he left me that day. I didn't contradict him, but I wondered. . . . I've wondered ever since. But he was Elvira's boy—I couldn't bring myself to say anything. Ah, well, you're a righteous woman, Jane Marple, and right must prevail. I'm sorry for his wife, though."

"So am I," said Miss Marple.

In the hall Pat Fortescue was waiting to say good-by.

"I wish you weren't going," she said. "I shall miss you."

"It's time for me to go," said Miss Marple. "I've finished what I came here to do. It hasn't been—altogether pleasant. But it's important, you know, that wickedness shouldn't triumph."

Pat looked puzzled.

"I don't understand."

"No, my dear. But perhaps you will someday. If I might venture to advise, if anything ever—goes wrong in your life—I think the happiest thing for you would be to go back to where you were happy as a child. Go back to Ireland, my dear. Horses and dogs. All that."

Pat nodded.

"Sometimes I wish I'd done just that when Freddy died. But if I had," her voice changed and softened, "I'd never have met Lance."

Miss Marple sighed.

"We're not staying here, you know," said Pat. "We're going back to East Africa as soon as everything's cleared up. I'm so glad."

"God bless you, dear child," said Miss Marple. "One needs a great deal of courage to get through life. I think you have it."

She patted the girl's hand and, releasing it, went through the front door to the waiting taxi.

ii.

Miss Marple reached home late that evening.

Kitty, the latest graduate from St. Faith's Home, let her in and greeted her with a beaming face.

"I've got a herring for your supper, miss. I'm so glad to see you home. You'll find everything very nice in the house. Regular spring cleaning I've had."

"That's very nice, Kitty. I'm glad to be home."

Six spider webs on the cornice, Miss Marple noted. These girls never raised their heads! She was none the less too kind to say so.

"Your letters is on the hall table, miss. And there's one as went to Daisymead by mistake. Always doing that, aren't they? Does look a bit alike, Dane and Daisy, and the writing's so bad I don't wonder this time. They've been away there and the house shut up. They only got back and sent it round today. Said as how they hoped it wasn't important."

Miss Marple picked up her correspondence. The letter to which Kitty had referred was on top of the others. A faint chord of remembrance stirred in Miss

Marple's mind at the sight of the blotted scrawled hand-writing. She tore it open.

Dear Madam,

I hope as you'll forgive me writing this but I really don't know what to do indeed I don't and I never meant no harm. Dear madam, you'll have seen the newspapers it was murder they say but it wasn't me that did it, not really because I would never do anything wicked like that and I know was how he woun't either. Albert, I mean. I'm telling this badly, but you see we met last summer and was going to be married only Bert hadn't got his rights, he'd been done out of them, swindled by this Mr. Fortescue who's dead. And Mr. Fortescue he just denied everything and of course everybody believed him and not Bert because he was rich and Bert was poor. But Bert had a friend who works in a place where they make these new drugs and there's what they call a truth drug you've read about it perhaps in the paper and it makes people speak the truth whether they want to or not. Bert was going to see Mr. Fortescue in his office on Oct. 31st, and taking a lawyer with him and I was to be sure to give him the drug at breakfast that morning and then it would work just right for when they came and he'd admit as all what Bert said was quite true. Well, madam, I put it in the marmalade but now he's dead and I think as how it must have been too strong but it wasn't Bert's fault because Bert would never do a thing like that but I can't tell the police because maybe they'd think Bert did it on purpose which I know he didn't. Oh, madam, I don't know what to do or what to say and the police are here in the house and it's awful and they ask you questions and look at you so stern and I don't know what to do and I haven't heard from Bert. Oh, madam, I don't like to ask it of you but if you could only come here and help me they'd listen to you and you were always so kind to me and, I didn't mean anything wrong and Bert didn't either. If you could only help us.

Yours respectfully,
Gladys Martin

P.S. I'm enclosing a snap of Bert and me. One of the boys took it at the camp and give it me. Bert doesn't know I've got it—he hates being snapped. But you can see, madam, what a nice boy he is.

Miss Marple, her lips pursed together, stared down at the photograph. The pair pictured there were looking at each other. Miss Marple's eyes went from Gladys's pathetic, adoring face, the mouth slightly open, to the other face—the dark, handsome, smiling face of Lance Fortescue.

The last words of the pathetic letter echoed in her mind:

You can see what a nice boy he is.

The tears rose in Miss Marple's eyes. Succeeding pity, there came anger—anger against a heartless killer.

And then, displacing both these emotions, there came a surge of triumph—the triumph some specialist might feel who has successfully reconstructed an extinct animal from a fragment of jawbone and a couple of teeth.

Agatha Christie's *favorite*

THE REMARKABLE MISS MARPLE

Everyone knows MISS JANE MARPLE—she's that elderly spinster lady whose innocent china-blue eyes hide a mind of steel. A mind that solves crimes—in all sorts of surprising ways.

Put a little mystery into your life—a Miss Jane Marple murder mystery by Agatha Christie from Pocket Books.

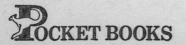

POCKET BOOKS